P9-CLD-966

Man in the Moon

Dotti Enderle

MAN
IN THE
MOON

DELACORTE PRESS

Published by Delacorte Press
an imprint of Random House Children's Books
a division of Random House, Inc.
New York

This is a work of fiction. All incidents and dialogue, and all characters with the
exception of some well-known historical and public figures, are products of the
author's imagination and are not to be construed as real. Where real-life historical
or public figures appear, the situations, incidents, and dialogues concerning those
persons are fictional and are not intended to depict actual events or to change the
fictional nature of the work. In all other respects, any resemblance to persons
living or dead is entirely coincidental.

Copyright © 2008 by Dotti Enderle
Illustrations copyright © 2008 by Kristina Swarner

All rights reserved.

Delacorte Press and colophon are registered trademarks of Random House, Inc.

Visit us on the Web! www.randomhouse.com/kids

Educators and librarians, for a variety of teaching tools,
visit us at www.randomhouse.com/teachers

Library of Congress Cataloging-in-Publication Data is available on request.
ISBN 978-0-385-73566-7 (trade)
ISBN 978-0-385-90554-1 (glb)

The text of this book is set in 12-point Goudy.
Printed in the United States of America
10 9 8 7 6 5 4 3 2 1
First Edition

Random House Children's Books
supports the First Amendment
and celebrates the right to read.

*No writer does it alone, and I'm no exception. A lot
of people helped make* Man in the Moon *shine.*

*I'd like to thank Elaine Trull and Adrienne Enderle
for reading it and encouraging me. A special thanks to
Vicki Sansum, who explained to me exactly how
Janine should relate to Mr. Lunas.*

*Many thanks to my editor, Stephanie Lane. And multiple
thanks to my agent, Erin Murphy, who helped me
through those early drafts and put her faith
in me and my work.*

Shine on!

Phase One—New Moon

I sat in the shadows of my bedroom, staring through the window screen. Except for an occasional lightning bug twinkling by, the night was black as molasses, and the air as thick. I prayed for just one breeze to blow through and cool the sweat on my face. But everything was still—dead still—like right before a storm.

My dog, Buddy, was laying outside, just under my window. I could hear him panting. Poor dog. He had no spit at all left on that long rough tongue of his. He'd probably found a cool spot in the dirt, or maybe he just took comfort in lying next to me, even if the wall did separate us.

I yawned. Buddy whimpered and rolled over. I could smell the dry dirt he'd stirred up from the flower bed. I leaned forward, pressing my head on the screen, trying to see what Buddy was up to.

That's when something moved in the corn-field. I heard it, just on the other side of the chicken coop. The corn shook for a moment, like someone trying to burrow his way beyond those gi-ant stalks. I sat still as a possum, listening in that direction. Buddy stopped panting. I couldn't see him, but I could sense he was alert.

The only noises were the crickets, and the dryflies crying for rain. And that pesky mosquito buzzing and sticking to my sweaty hair. The corn-field sometimes swayed and crackled when a strong wind sang through. But there was nothing out there tonight to move that corn—no breeze. Nothing. Except an animal . . . or a person?

It moved again. Buddy shot toward the chicken coop yapping and barking, his dry throat making him sound like an old man with the whooping cough.

I slipped out of my room and hurried to the back door to see what it was. I had to tiptoe when I got to the screened-in porch. Mama and Daddy were sleeping out there again tonight. They'd propped a portable fan on one of Mama's plant stands with a long black extension cord snaked under the back door to the kitchen plug. They could barely take the Texas heat during a normal summer, but this July had temperatures soaring higher than the stars. And the humidity had us all feeling like chewed gum. I had heard on the news a few months ago that President Kennedy wants to send a man to the moon. Daddy said if he does, he hopes he'll install a giant air conditioner up there and point it straight at us.

I tried to see out back, but the darkness blinded me. No porch light or moonlight. I heard Buddy roll off one of his low, menacing growls, telling whoever or whatever was out there that he meant to tear 'em up if they took another step. I heard the shuffling of the cornstalks again, then silence. A minute later Buddy came trotting back to the house like nothing was wrong.

But something *was* wrong. I could sense it. Feel it. Someone was out there in the corn, all right. And I had a feeling he was staring right at me.

☾

After a restless night, I woke to a yellow sun slanting through the crevices. I headed into the kitchen, where Mama sat at the table, studying the wet brown leaves that had blobbed together in her teacup. Ricky was perched next to her, already dressed in blue shorts and a plaid cotton shirt.

"You's a sleepyhead," he said, dragging his spoon across the sugar on his milky toast.

I answered him with a yawn.

"Janine?" Mama said, never looking up from her cup.

I knew a question would follow.

"Did you go outside last night?"

"No." That wasn't a lie. 'Cause I only *looked* outside.

"Somebody was out there."

The way she said it made my skin crawl. Then she sighed. "And we know it wasn't Ricky."

Ricky squinted his eyes and gave me a gap-toothed grin. He knocked out his front tooth falling out of a tree two years ago, and Mama swears it'll never grow back in.

I grabbed a chair and plopped down. It made a grating screech as I pulled myself up to the table. "What makes you think somebody was outside?" I was careful with the question. I wanted to hear the answer, but at the same time, I was afraid it might scare me to death. I just knew Mama was going to say she saw some trampled corn. That would mean someone really had been snooping around our place.

She shifted her eyes toward me. "When I went out to feed Buddy there were footprints on the steps. Footprints, not shoeprints. You're the only one here that spends the entire summer barefoot."

"How come I can't go barefoot?" Ricky asked, kicking a sandaled foot in the air.

"You know why," Mama answered. She stared back down into her cup.

I'm not convinced Ricky really did know why. I know I didn't! He was sick, that was for sure, but Mama never would let him do the things other kids did. He could only go outside at certain times, and he was never allowed to go without shoes. Mama wouldn't let a fan blow directly on him, even when he slept. I guess that's why he always looked like he had a fever. I asked Daddy once what was wrong with Ricky, and all he said was "He was born with his gizzard backwards." That was Daddy's way of protecting me from the truth, whatever it was.

But when Ricky and I played together, he acted like anybody else. He didn't faint or swoon or puke. Just an occasional nosebleed or cough. Sometimes he sat down tired. But then, so did I.

Mama set the cup aside and rubbed her eyes.

"What'd you see?" I asked, leaning on my elbows and gazing at her plump face.

"Same thing I always see. No money. No jobs. The world going to hell in a handbasket. Oh, and a little girl who won't admit that she went outside after bedtime."

"That's bullcorn!" I shouted, slapping my hands on the table.

"Watch your language," Mama warned.

"I swear, Mama, it wasn't me."

She gave me that stare, like her eyes were firing bullets. No words, just a hard stare.

"It's not fair! I get blamed for durn near everything. How do you know it wasn't Ricky? It coulda been!"

Ricky's head shot up from his breakfast and his mouth went slack. "It wasn't me."

"Don't smart-mouth me," Mama said to me, her eyes still firing. "And apologize to your brother. He don't need the aggravation."

"Sorry," I said to him, not meaning it. I think I've spent most of my life apologizing to him about

7

something. I can't remember a time when Ricky wasn't the favorite, but I did see a picture once, from when I was a baby. It was just me and Mama and Daddy. Everyone was smiling. More than smiling. Mama and Daddy were grinning like I was the best thing to happen since ice cream. But just like all little brothers, Ricky had to come along and ruin it for me.

I forced my lip out of a pout and continued. "Anyway, I heard Buddy barking last night, so maybe it was a stranger at the back porch."

Mama let out a fake laugh. "What would a stranger want around here?"

I shrugged.

"Could've been a robber, huh?" she said. "Got up to the house and realized we didn't have a danged thing to steal." Mama shook her head and let out another phony laugh.

I didn't like that talk. Even in the stifling heat, a chill prickled me just thinking it could have been a robber.

"You gonna eat anything?" Mama asked me,

picking up Ricky's plate. He'd eaten only the inside of his milky toast, leaving the soggy crust to wilt in the remaining milk.

My stomach grumbled. "I'll have a boiled egg, I guess."

I heard the clinking of dishes in the sink; then Mama turned on the faucet. "You better go gather some from the henhouse then, 'cause we ain't got any in the icebox."

I suddenly lost my appetite for a boiled egg. That would mean I'd have to go out to our chicken coop, right there in front of the cornfield—a little too close to whoever was spying on us last night.

☽

The sun was unforgiving that day. If I'd taken a notion to eat an egg after all, I probably wouldn't have needed to cook it. The earth was an oven, baking us to the bone. Mama let Ricky go outside with me late that afternoon on the condition that he stay in the shade, close to the house. But we knew Mama pretty well. Soon she'd be cleaning and sewing and she wouldn't know what we were up to.

"Let's go out to the truck and dig through the junk," I said.

Ricky lit up like a sparkler. "I'll race ya!"

Before I could protest, he was flying across the pasture, his arms flapping like wings. Buddy chased at his heels. I ran too, but even though I have tough feet, I had to dodge the cow pies and bull nettles, so Ricky beat me by a mile.

"Loser!" he said, leaning against the old flat-bed truck.

I couldn't let him get away with that. "I let you win."

"Yeah, you say that every time."

" 'Cause it's true every time." Actually, it wasn't. For a kid with a backwards gizzard, Ricky could run like the wind.

We walked around the truck and started digging through the heap of trash. We didn't know whose truck it was, but someone had abandoned it on the property next to our farm. The cab was rusted out and filthy, and the tires had been taken off ages ago. But the wooden bed in the back had a mountain of trash just waiting for us to explore. We'd found some pretty neat stuff here before: old dishes, a rickety baby carriage, a dirty coin purse with a nickel caught in the lining. It seemed like Christmas every time we came out here. We even found an old wooden leg once. It was splintered and worn, and the pointed leather foot had some dark stains. But it was an awesome find. I wanted to bring it home to make a spook house in the barn, but Mama said to leave it be. A wooden leg would bring bad luck.

I climbed on top of the truck, then pulled Ricky up. We had to be careful not to step on anything rusty. Mama said we'd get lockjaw and starve to death from not being able to open our mouths. A heck of a way to die.

It didn't take long for us to find something to play with. Ricky dug out a broken swim flipper, and I found a greasy tennis ball. I wiped it off on the wooden truck bed as best I could; then Ricky and I played a long game of Swat. I pitched the ball to him and he swatted it with the flipper. Sometimes he'd hold it to the side like a baseball bat, and sometimes he'd hold it flat out in front of him and swat the ball straight up. No matter which way, he was pretty good at it. When it was my turn, I barely hit the thing—maybe once out of ten times. When I'd miss, Buddy would grab the ball, and we'd have to tug it out of his slobbery mouth.

"You swat like a girl!" Ricky yelled.

"Well, you look like one!" I yelled back.

Ricky tossed the ball up high and caught it himself. "Guess what?" he said. "I'm going to ask Daddy if I can have a go-cart."

That was the dumbest thing I'd ever heard. "Uh-huh. And I'm going to ask him for a mansion in Hollywood."

"No, really," Ricky said, tossing the ball toward me.

I swung and missed . . . again. "You're full of beans. Daddy won't buy a go-cart unless we can eat it for supper. Or did you forget? He ain't got a job!"

"I'm going to ask anyway," Ricky said.

"What do you want a stupid go-cart for? You ain't got nobody to race."

"Ain't you ever heard of racing time?" he asked.

How fast did he think a go-cart would move? "You ain't got a stopwatch, either."

He looked down at the ground and kicked the dirt. "I just want a go-cart, okay? I want to zoom . . . like a rocket."

I wasn't sure what he meant, but it probably had a lot to do with being cooped up on this farm. At least he had an excuse. But why on earth did I have to be stuck here all the time? My gizzard was just fine, thank you. Only I knew the answer. I was stuck here because of Ricky. Everything is because of Ricky. I don't think I could count all the days I wished I could just take off running and never stop.

I picked up the ball and threw it back to him, but it dropped at his feet. His eyes bulged and he froze where he was. A second later he started to cough.

I knew I should've brought a jar of water! He heaved and wrestled with a dry cough that sounded like sand might come poofing out of his throat.

"Ricky, are you all right?"

He dropped the ball and took refuge under the truck bed, where it was nice and shady. He continued to hack like something was stuck in him. I wasn't sure what to do. This was one of those times when I wanted to help, to make things all right, but as usual I was nothing but a helpless lump.

The sun was an orange blister hiding behind the summer haze. It had to be close to dinnertime. I reached under the truck to pull Ricky out. I figured I could carry him back to the house. A thin line of blood oozed out of his nose.

"It's okay," he said, pushing me away. His cough had slowed to an occasional spasm. He wiped his bloody nose on the back of his hand. "It's okay," he said again. I wasn't sure who he was trying to convince.

Buddy was pacing and whining. He could sense that something was wrong.

I reached in for Ricky again, and this time he let me help him out from under the truck. "We better get back."

We limped across the pasture, him from his illness, me from just being worn out.

I wasn't as careful as I should have been, and by the time I got to the back steps, there must have been at least fifteen sticker burrs stuck in my feet. Some were poked in pretty deep. I sat down and started picking them out. I noticed Ricky tiptoeing away, craning his neck to see behind the chicken coop.

"What are you looking for?" I asked.

Ricky whipped around real quick and looked back at me. "Nothing. I thought I saw something in the corn."

I plucked the rest of the stickers out real fast, stabbing my fingers on a few of the prickles.

Mama came out on the steps and gave us a suspicious look. "Ricky! You're as red as blazes, child.

And I bet you're just as hot, too. Weren't you staying in the shade like I said?"

I could tell that Ricky's brown eyes were searching for a lie, but he never was any good at fibbing. And besides, what difference did it make? Mama never had the heart to punish him because of his gizzard. I would be the one to get a whupping with a switch. Before he answered, she noticed the smeared blood under his nose.

"Lawsy! You're bleeding again, baby. Let's get you to bed."

Ricky didn't say a word as Mama threw her arm around his shoulder to lead him inside. Just then, Daddy's old blue Chevy came crunching down the gravel drive. Ricky broke loose from Mama, and we hurried to greet Daddy as he stepped out of the car. He squeezed us both up in a tight bear hug and gave us each a big kiss on the cheek. The kiss was one of those loud smacks that ended with a puckered *pop!* I could smell beer on his breath and knew he hadn't spent the whole day out looking for work.

He walked to the house with his head hanging a bit. That was his way of telling Mama that he hadn't had any luck.

We all headed in for dinner, first Mama, then Ricky, then Daddy. I was the last one to go in, but not before I heard something moving in the corn-field again. I looked back to see Buddy disappear behind some tall stalks.

Phase Two—Waxing Crescent

The next couple of days were pretty quiet, except for all that rustling in the corn. I thought maybe an animal had gotten trapped in there and was trying to get out. Buddy spent a lot of time snooping around, but he always trotted back from the field with a satisfied look, like someone had just fed him a T-bone. I wondered why Mama and Daddy didn't hear the rustling. It got louder every day. I thought about going in to investigate it myself but was just too doggone scared. It might be one of those weird things like on *The Twilight Zone*, and I sure didn't want Rod Serling introducing a show about me.

I decided I'd just spend my days inside. Ricky couldn't go out anyway, and I hated always playing by myself. Mama was still in a tizzy over him getting overheated and would barely allow him near the window. I stayed in my room mostly, listening to the marches of John Philip Sousa and twirling my baton like I was one of those glittery girls during the halftime show at a UT game. They're lucky, getting to perform at football games in places like Arkansas and Oklahoma. That's why I practice a lot. I couldn't throw the baton in the air or over my shoulder because if Mama'd found out I was twirling in the house, she'd have switched me good. I just wish we didn't live so far out in the country so I could practice twirling with my best friends, Debbie and Cheryl. But Daddy's gone all day in our car, and it takes forty-five minutes to get to civilization. And they can't come visit me because Mama said they'd just be spreading germs to Ricky. Ugh! They're probably having a hi-ho time this summer doing fun stuff like painting their nails or going to the drive-in movie. I'd give anything to go to the drive-in.

It was late in the day when Daddy came home, his Chevy kicking up dust with its back tires. He sat down to dinner with that downhearted look on his face.

"How was job hunting?" Mama asked. "Any bites?"

Daddy shrugged. "Not even a nibble. And I drove all the way to Austin."

"Austin!" Mama shook her head as she slapped a pile of creamed potatoes on her plate. "Well, something's got to turn up soon."

I hated seeing Daddy look so low. "I bet President Kennedy is gonna do something real soon," I said, hoping to cheer him up. Daddy had been so happy last November when President Kennedy got elected. Lots of people cheered. Even Mama had clapped her hands, saying prosperous times were on the horizon. But that was back then.

Daddy stabbed some green beans with his fork.

"Janine, if there is one thing on this God-given earth you need to learn, it's that you can't rely on politicians to solve your problems. Heck, you can't rely on anyone. You got to make it happen yourself."

"Well, I sure hope you make it happen soon," Mama said, "'cause we're heading for the poorhouse fast."

I sure wish President Kennedy would work faster. Those prosperous times took one look at us and sank down out of sight.

☾

Mama and Ricky and I sat on the back steps around nightfall, hoping to catch a cool breeze. Daddy was out in the barn, milking our two cows.

Ricky sat doll-like, limp and lifeless. He'd been to the doctor that afternoon, and those visits always did something strange to him. Mama looked drained too. She said that for a sickly boy, Ricky had a lot of fight in him when that nurse came in with the shot needle. It plumb tuckered her out just holding him down.

The sky had turned a lovely shade of velvety purple, and the moon was only a sliver on the horizon. A few faded stars were just beginning to twinkle when we heard some commotion behind the chicken coop. Buddy ran back there without barking, so we figured whatever it was couldn't be too threatening. But right then, a figure came loping around the chickens, heading our way.

A thin ghost of a man trudged his way up our backyard, wearing baggy gray pants and a yellowed white shirt. His hat was cocked back on his head. He was as skinny as Mama's crochet hook and his shoes flopped when he walked. If I hadn't known better, I would have sworn our scarecrow had come to life and was joining us for a sit.

Mama disappeared into the house, then hurried back out holding a shotgun. "What're you doing in our corn patch?" she asked, resting the gun steady on her shoulder.

The man raised his wiry arms, just like the fugitives on TV, and a small crescent of a smile lined his face. "Is James here?"

Mama lowered the gun. "You know my husband?"

He removed his hat. "Yes, ma'am."

Ricky and I were huddled together against the house. I couldn't help wondering if this weedy-looking old man wasn't the one who'd been stirring in the corn for the past week.

Daddy walked up about then, holding the milk bucket. He set it down and slowly walked toward the stranger, his head tilted, studying the man's face. He had a questioning look that made his eyebrows join together in the middle. "Mr. Lunas?"

The scarecrow man's crescent smile grew bigger. "One and the same."

Daddy clapped his hands together and whooped like an Indian. "Lunas! You old cuss! You haven't changed a bit!"

Yuck! This man's always looked like this?

Daddy went up and threw his arm around Mr. Lunas's shoulder. I was afraid the old guy might crack and crumble to the ground like a broken

24

potato chip. But his bones must have been stronger than they looked because he and Daddy walked up together, grinning like mice in a cheese factory.

"Mr. Lunas, this is my wife, Adele."

Mr. Lunas nodded his head. "Ma'am."

Daddy faced us. "And these are my kids, Janine and Ricky."

"My, my," Mr. Lunas said. "You two look so much alike, you must be twins."

"Nuh-uh! I'm a whole year older than Ricky!" I always have to set people straight on that bullcorn.

"Almost to the day," Daddy added. "Adele, I told you about Mr. Lunas. He saved my life during the war."

Mama's face lit up in recognition; then she slid the shotgun back behind her skirt.

"It's a pleasure to meet you, Mr. Lunas. Come on in for a glass of iced tea."

We all followed.

As we sat at the kitchen table, Mama filled Mr. Lunas's tea glass. He gulped the tea down like he'd just stepped out of the desert. Mama poured him another.

"So how did you find me?" Daddy asked, leaning forward on the table with his arms crossed.

"It wasn't hard." Mr. Lunas drained that glass of tea too.

"Kids, you should thank Mr. Lunas. If it hadn't been for him, you wouldn't even be here."

Ricky and I looked at each other. "Thank you," Ricky said, kinda quiet. I stayed silent. I wasn't saying anything until I had the facts. But I swear, I'd never seen Daddy so excited about seeing someone. I thought he was going to jump up and start tap dancing any minute. "So what happened?" I finally asked.

Daddy got that look in his eyes—like he was going to reveal the secret to some magic trick, or the location of a buried treasure. "WW Two," he started. "I took a couple of bullets from a German soldier."

"Where'd you take them?" Ricky asked. I nudged Ricky to hush.

"In the gut," Daddy said. "I lay there, face-down, my mouth gritty with dirt. I could hear gunfire all around, and grenades popping like firecrackers. Only it wasn't the Fourth of July. It was Judgment Day for me. Or so I thought. Blood had pooled all around me, making a muddy mess stickier than a pigsty. My belly burned and ached. I couldn't move."

Ricky groaned and wiggled in his chair.

"I knew I was a goner. Then I looked up, and there was this puny soldier grinning down at me like the Man in the Moon. 'What're you grinning at, fool?' I asked him. Just before I blacked out, I heard him say 'It ain't your time to go.'

"When I woke up I was in the medical ward, and there he was, sitting by my cot. He'd drug me through all that flying ammo and got me to some help. And I swear, if he hadn't, the army would've been sending me home in a wooden box."

An involuntary shudder shook me. I looked over at Mr. Lunas, who was staring at his empty tea glass and sporting that crescent grin. He looked like the story had embarrassed him some. On that skinny, pale face of his appeared a couple of cherry dots flaring at the cheeks. But for the life of me, I couldn't figure out how a man as scrawny as Mr. Lunas could drag anybody more than a couple of feet without giving out and falling over himself.

"Yep," Daddy went on, "his encouragement is what kept me going." Daddy looked thoughtful for a moment, then asked, "What unit were you with again?"

Mr. Lunas jerked his head up like he was caught off guard. "Uh—medical corps."

"Oh yeah," Daddy said, nodding.

"Well, we're certainly grateful," Mama said, filling Mr. Lunas's glass for the third time. "Can I get you something to eat?"

"That'd be right kind of you," Mr. Lunas said sweetly.

"That's the least we can do!" Daddy blurted.

Mama got up and went to the pantry. She took out a jar of pickled pigs' feet and grabbed some left-over biscuits off the counter. She set them on the table, and he dug in like a man starving to death. He didn't even wait for a fork! Just grabbed them pigs' feet right out of the jar, letting the vinegar drip all over Mama's table. He chomped like Buddy, gnawing the pork and cramming the biscuits into his mouth. Then he washed them down with the tea, gulping it in giant swallows. As he set the glass down, ice chinked against the sides. I'm surprised he didn't devour those ice cubes, too! Then he looked at Mama and nodded.

"I guess you were hungry," Daddy said with a laugh.

"Guess I was," Mr. Lunas echoed.

There was a minute of awkward silence; then Daddy asked, "You need a place to stay?"

Mr. Lunas shook his head like Daddy was

offering to give him his car or something. "No, no. I wouldn't want to put you folks to any trouble."

"No trouble at all." Daddy placed his hand on Mr. Lunas's arm. "Stay as long as you like."

Mama shot Daddy a look that would have sent Buddy running with his tail between his legs.

But Daddy never was one to be bullied, so he ignored it and said, "We got a nice cozy couch if you don't mind an occasional spring poking your rear."

Mr. Lunas chuckled. "I'm obliged."

Mama went to the linen closet for an extra pillow and sheet. On her way back through the kitchen, she glanced at Ricky and me. "It's past your bedtime."

We learned a long time ago not to argue about that. We sailed off, shouting, "Good night, and glad to meet you!"

☾

I woke up later that night, my body wet from sweat and my shorties sticking to me all over. I went into the kitchen for a drink of water. The house was still except for the creaking of the linoleum under my feet. I opened the icebox, letting the light pour out and the coolness wash over me. The water pitcher felt dewy and cold, and I drank right from it.

After closing the icebox door, I thought about Mr. Lunas, just on the other side of the wall, sleeping on the couch. I should have hurried on out of there, back to my bed, but I couldn't help wanting another peek at that strange-looking fellow. As skinny as he was, I figured our couch just might swallow him up. Without making a sound . . . without taking a breath . . . without even blinking . . . I peeped around the kitchen door into the living room.

It was dark and still; not even a shadow was visible. But I could see the sheet folded up on the end of the couch, and the pillow still fluffed and untouched. Mr. Lunas wasn't there.

I started having creepy notions that he was lurking right behind me, just like the Booger Man, but I glanced over my shoulder and that put my mind at ease. Now, where had that old skeleton gone?

I crossed to the living room window and looked out, thinking I might see him on the front porch, petting Buddy or something. I saw him all right, but it was the darnedest sight in the world. Mr. Lunas lay flat on his back on the ground, arms stretched out at his sides, legs sprawled open. Buddy lay next to him, breathing peacefully.

At first I thought Mr. Lunas must be dead, his eyes staring up at the sky, frozen and still. I was one clock-tick away from screaming my lungs out. Then I saw his hand move. He reached over and petted Buddy, and Buddy scootched in closer to him.

Those eyes. Those lifeless eyes were drinking in something from above. I squatted down to try to see what was up there that was so fascinating. All I saw was the moon, slim and trim as a toenail. I rushed out of there and got back to bed in a hurry.

Sweat or no sweat, I covered up tight, my mind as tangled as a cobweb.

All sorts of notions ran through my brain. Why would a man stay up at night, looking plumb dead, yet happy at the same time? Mama says there's no such thing as monsters, but I'm not so sure. I should have checked to see if he had fangs. Could Mr. Lunas be a vampire?

Phase Three—First Quarter

It turns out, Mr. Lunas wasn't a vampire at all. I saw him walking around in the daylight, eating everything he could get his hands on. Mama said Daddy needed to find a job fast, just to support that old man's appetite. He could really put it away!

I decided to avoid him. I still hadn't gotten over him laying out on the ground at night, staring off into the sky like some lunatic. I took to propping a chair under my doorknob before bed, just in case he wasn't in his right mind. I sure didn't want him getting in.

It was easy to stay out of his way for the next few days. He spent the whole weekend following Daddy around. They drove off in the Chevy a lot, and late at night they sat behind the chicken coop, drinking beer. Of course they waited until Mama was asleep. She didn't allow alcohol around the house, so Daddy had to sneak it whenever he could.

He'd put off looking for a job for nearly a week and couldn't put it off anymore. He was gone when I went in for breakfast. Only Mama and Mr. Lunas sat at the kitchen table. Ricky was still in his room, snoozing.

"So what do you see in that teacup, Adele?" Mr. Lunas asked, his breakfast plate clean as a whistle.

Mama raised her eyebrows, but not her eyes. "James needs work. Ricky needs an operation. I need rest." She didn't say anything about me. *So what else is new?*

Mr. Lunas gave off one of his glowing grins. "Do you really need tea leaves to tell you that?"

"You asked me what I saw in the cup, not what it tells me."

Mr. Lunas crossed his arms and leaned on the table. "What does it *tell* you?"

Mama's face grew dark and somber. "That something big is going to happen. Something we can't avoid. It tells me that my family will be turned upside down and cattiwhompus. It's big, Mr. Lunas. Real big—like the seven plagues in the Bible." Mama caught me staring and shushed up real fast.

Mr. Lunas chuckled and pointed down into the cup. "I wouldn't put much stock in what those tea leaves say, Adele." Then he pointed to his heart. "This is what you need to be listening to." He scooted away from the table and went out the back door.

Mama shook her head. "What I didn't tell him was that the first plague would probably be famine. If that old coot keeps eating like he does, the rest of us are going to starve to death."

Ricky dragged into the kitchen, rubbing his

eyes and scratching himself. "Mr. Lunas is getting fat," he said, looking toward the back door.

"I wonder why!" Mama said, throwing her hands in the air. "Sit down and I'll see if he left anything for you to eat." She took the last honey muffin from the baking tin and handed it to Ricky with a bottle of white syrup. "Grab a plate," she said, nodding toward me.

I did. She put the muffin on it and handed it to Ricky. *I sure hope Mr. Lunas is getting fat*, I thought, looking down at my toothpick legs and knotty knees. *'Cause he should get something good out of eating my breakfast.* Just then Mama pulled another tin of muffins out of the oven.

"I hid 'em," she said, smiling at me.

Ricky mashed up his muffin with a fork and poured on a river of syrup. It looked like something that'd already been chewed and spit out. "Can I go outside today?"

Mama stopped for a minute, like she was considering it. "I think it's just too hot out there. It ain't ten o'clock yet and I bet you could already fry an egg on the sidewalk."

"If we did, Mr. Lunas would just eat it," I said.

Ricky laughed so hard muffin mush leaked out of his mouth.

"Stay inside today," Mama said. "It's too hot for both of you."

I wasn't going to argue with that. Unless, of course, Mr. Lunas decided to spend the day inside.

☾

Ricky and I did stay in. We hid in our cave most of the day. It's not a real cave. Just the narrow space under the piano. We played cards, and dinosaurs, and I Spy, and a bunch of other silly games that we made up ourselves—like sitting on the piano pedals to see if our butts could hold both of them down at once. After three tries, I almost did it, but I ended up with a sore heinie instead. We finally crawled out at three o'clock to watch afternoon cartoons.

We were sprawled on the living room floor when Mr. Lunas came in and sat on the couch. As he was getting fatter, his smile was getting fuller. "You kids been having a good day?"

I wanted to keep watching cartoons and not say anything. Pretend like we didn't hear him. But Ricky rolled over and grinned. "Mr. Lunas! Are you going to watch cartoons with us?"

"Sure," he said, crossing his legs.

I didn't say a word. Instead I got up slowly, deciding I'd skip cartoons and sneak off to my room. As I passed by the couch, Mr. Lunas reached out and grabbed my arm. I froze on the spot, my guts turning upside down.

"You know, Janine," he said, "you don't have to be afraid. I won't bite you."

I sort of had the feeling that he really wouldn't, but I still couldn't get that vision out of my head: Him laying on the ground with that crazy look in his eyes, staring up at the sky. But why? Could Mr. Lunas have been a hobo who just liked sleeping outside? Or maybe it was too durned hot for him to sleep inside. Mama and Daddy sleep on the porch, and that's kinda like outside. He must've had some good reason.

It took a lot of doing, but I forced myself to smile at him. "I'm just going to go help Mama shell peas."

Darn! Those words just shot out of my mouth without me thinking about them first. Now I was really mad at myself. But I kept my word and spent the afternoon shelling peas.

That night we sat under a half-moon, Daddy whistling and Mama fanning herself with a magazine. Ricky rolled a toy car around in the dirt, making zooming noises under his breath, while I got lost in a daydream about when I grow up to be a movie star. I could see myself on that big drive-in screen, while Cheryl and Debbie sat in a car watching me perform.

Mr. Lunas sat in the lawn chair with his head tilted back, Buddy at his feet. He told Mama he was working a kink out of his neck, but I knew better. His gaze was fixed on that velvet sky. The stars filled it like spilled diamonds, and although only half of the moon was showing, I could see the shadow of the other half, waiting its turn to shine.

"Can I have a go-cart?" Ricky asked, rolling his toy car over Daddy's worn-out brown shoe.

Daddy held his sides and laughed like Milton Berle had just got pied in the face. "Son, as soon as I strike oil, I'll get you that go-cart."

Ricky flipped the toy over and rolled the wheels with his palm. "Can't we use Green Stamps?"

"No!" Mama said sharply. "We need those Green Stamps for an emergency."

Daddy winked. "Yeah, like an emergency bedspread or chicken fryer."

Mama gave him a bitter look.

Mr. Lunas kept staring up, even as he spoke. "Ricky, a go-cart sounds like a fine vehicle."

"Too fine," Daddy said. "He might as well ask for a Cadillac."

Ricky just slumped a little and murmured,

"Zoom." No oomph at all, just "zoom." It's a strange word to hear when there's no meaning attached. Kind of like Ricky was saying it while falling down a well.

Just then a dog howled in the distance and both Buddy and Mr. Lunas perked up.

"I wonder what that crazy old hound's howling about," Daddy said, taking a sip of iced tea.

Mr. Lunas tapped on the arm of his chair. "Do you know why dogs bark at the moon?"

No one answered because he was looking at me. I had no choice but to speak up. "No sir, I don't."

"Because they're smarter than people," he said.

What a bunch of bullcorn! Dogs, smarter than people? Then why don't dogs go to school or get jobs or drive cars? Why doesn't Buddy sleep in the house while we sleep in the dirt? Why don't dogs dip *themselves* in creosote to get rid of fleas? And I swear I've never once seen a dog open his own box of Gravy Train. Of course I didn't say none of that. I simply asked, "How are dogs smarter than people?"

43

"Over the years, people have complicated their lives," Mr. Lunas said, looking back up at the stars. "In their quest to better themselves, they've forgotten where they came from. How they got here, and why they came at all. They invented ink and paper and pens to keep track, but somewhere in the distant past, they lost all memory. Dogs don't need history books. They know what's important. They're filled with memories of their early existence, from the most vicious wolf to the tamest poodle. They know something people don't."

Mama fanned herself harder and rolled her eyes at me. I guess she thought Mr. Lunas was a loony, too.

Daddy stretched. "Well, I may not be as smart as a dog, but I know when mosquitoes are winning a battle with my hide. I'm going in."

We all gathered ourselves up and walked to the back porch. All except Mr. Lunas. He stretched his legs out in front of him like he was going to camp out in that chair. A breeze blew through, shaking the cornstalks. He closed his eyes and smiled like that sound was a fancy orchestra playing his favorite song. The whole business gave me the chills, even though it must have been eighty-five degrees outside. Mr. Lunas was the oddest fellow I'd ever met.

I didn't bother propping a chair under my doorknob that night. I sat with the light out, looking through my bedroom window. I could see Mr. Lunas, still leaning back in the chair. Buddy would circle him a few times, put his front paws up on his lap, then go to circling him again, like he wanted his attention or was trying to tell him something. Mr. Lunas never looked down at Buddy. He'd just reach his hand out and rub Buddy's fur. Buddy would pant and whine a little. He'd nudge at Mr. Lunas, like a puppy wanting to play. I'd never seen Buddy take to someone the way he did this silly-looking old man. Maybe it was because Mr. Lunas thought dogs were smarter than people and Buddy could sense that. Who knows? But I did know one thing for sure. If a dog likes somebody, he can't be all *that* bad.

My eyes started drooping, so I crawled into bed. The night was too hot for covers. I lay there looking out the window at the fireflies with their little searchlights blinking. A million crickets sang through the pasture. A couple of June bugs bounced into the window screen, and just as I dozed off I heard something that froze my blood again. In the five years we'd owned Buddy, I'd heard him bark, growl, and whimper. But tonight he did something I've never heard him do. He howled at the moon.

Phase Four—Waxing Gibbous

The moon was getting rounder, and so was Mr. Lunas. Mama took to hiding food like a squirrel storing nuts for the winter. I could hear her and Daddy arguing late at night. Mama would say that Mr. Lunas was a freeloader and that he had to go. Daddy would jump back at her, insisting that Mr. Lunas was a war hero who deserved our respect and our food. He'd tell Mama that once he got a job, she wouldn't be so tense. Then she'd start off on why hadn't he found a job yet, and that digging ditches was respectable work too, why didn't he do that? That's about when I'd cover my head with a pillow to block it all out.

I stopped being curious about Mr. Lunas. No sense looking out the bedroom window. He was out there, night after night. Sometimes he sat, sometimes he stood. But his fascination with the moon and sky never changed. It just wasn't right for a grown man to act the way he did. What the heck did he see up there that we didn't? I craned my neck, trying to look up too. The window screen pressed hard against my forehead, and I could only stretch it a tiny bit. I couldn't see whatever it was that Mr. Lunas saw, but I was really aching to. Maybe tomorrow I'd ask him.

When I woke up, the sky was hidden behind gray clouds. The air smelled as damp as the laundry that Mama had hung out on the line. The temperature must have been ten degrees cooler, which made Ricky's grin almost as big as Mr. Lunas's growing belly. He nudged me and said, "I bet Mama lets me go outside today."

Mama stood in her bedroom, ironing clothes.

She had the radio tuned to the hillbilly station, and the music crackled each time the sky rumbled from the distant storm.

Ricky put on his "Please, Mama?" face and looked at her with big eyes.

"It's cool outside today, Mama. You feel it?"

Mama guided the iron over the pillowcase like we were invisible. Her forehead was beaded with sweat, even though a gusty wind caused her bedroom curtains to wave and flap. Ricky gave me a look and shrugged.

Mama sighed. "Go on! I have to hurry and finish this ironing before it comes a storm. I don't want to get electrocuted."

As we ran out of her room we heard her call, "But get yourselves back in here before the first drop falls, you hear me?"

We scampered out like two rabbits racing for cabbage. We passed Mr. Lunas, sitting on the back porch. He'd gained so much weight that he filled the whole chair.

"What're you young 'uns up to today?"

Ricky bounced and jumped like he'd been tied down for a month. "I get to play outside!" The word *outside* echoed through the brown pasture.

"Good for you," Mr. Lunas said. He tapped his foot and strummed his fingers on the arm of the chair. Mama's radio was turned too low for us to hear, so I couldn't help wondering what kind of song was playing in his head.

Ricky and I raced to the shade tree, Ricky tagging it first.

"Beat ya," he said, leaning forward, hands on hips.

I rolled my eyes at him. "I let you win."

"Uh-unh," he said, not buying it. He swallowed a deep breath, then let it out slow. "Janine, Daddy ain't ever going to buy me a go-cart."

"I told you so, didn't I?"

"Yeah," he said, looking sassy. "That's why I'm gonna build one."

I swear that boy had mush for brains. "Bullcorn. You can't build a go-cart. You don't know how."

"Yes, I do," he said, his skinny little body bouncing like a puppet.

"And what are you going to make it out of?"

Ricky didn't say a word. He just looked at the old flatbed truck sitting in the pasture.

"Why, that ain't nothing but a bunch of junk!"

"Right," he said. "But I bet there's enough junk piled there to put together a go-cart."

I shook my head. I didn't know how he could possibly make a go-cart out of a heap of trash. "What are you going to use for a motor?"

"It don't need a motor, silly. We'll glide down the hill out front, just like we used to do with that old cardboard box Daddy left in the barn."

I have to admit, that cardboard box was a lot of fun, even though it was a bumpy ride without much to hold on to. "Let's go!"

As soon as we started running, Buddy came loping behind. I was happy to see him. For a while there, I thought he'd become Mr. Lunas's dog.

The sky was getting darker, but we didn't care.

It only made the air cooler. I just knew God wouldn't let it rain while we were on a mission to find go-cart pieces. We'd spent too many days inside. He had to know that.

Ricky didn't waste any time climbing onto the truck. A piece of wire caught in the toe of his sandals, but he jerked it off and threw it to the side. He dug into that trash, reaching in and flinging things off like there was gold buried underneath. "Here!" he said, pulling up a long flat board. "We can use this." He leaned over and tossed it to the ground.

I started searching too, but I had no clue what to look for. I knew that Ricky had his go-cart designed in his head, and if I tried showing him what I thought would make a good one, he'd probably laugh and accuse *me* of having mush for brains. I figured it was safest to ask. "What do we need to build it?"

"Boards and wheels. Like these!" He pulled out the frame of an old baby buggy. The four rubber wheels still looked good, even though the spokes were freckled with brown rust. He tossed it on top of the board.

We worked for a good fifteen minutes with the clouds threatening to cry on us. I hurried, wondering what Mama would do to me if I brought Ricky home soaking wet.

Finally Ricky said, "That should be enough. I think Daddy has some rope in the barn."

Rope? Why the heck did we need rope for a go-cart? I nodded like I knew what he was talking about. I didn't want him to take time explaining it while the sky decided to let loose. We piled the boards on top of the buggy frame and scooted it across the pasture. The wheels were too rusty to roll, so it made long ridges in the dirt. Every once in a while it'd get caught on a clump of weeds and we'd have to lift it over. Buddy marched along next to us, his fluffy tail waving like a flag.

As we got to the barn, the buggy bumped against a knot of dirt that was harder than a brick. The boards shifted and almost fell. I jerked my foot up to brace the buggy so it wouldn't tilt. But that was a huge mistake. I caught my sole on a jagged piece of metal that was jutting out, and it cut a big gash right across the bottom of my foot.

"Shoot!" I yelled, dropping on my bottom and cradling my foot. It stung like I'd stuck it in a hornet's nest. Blood oozed up, then dripped down. I couldn't believe it. I'd been so careful not to step on the sticker patch, and now this.

"Can you make it to the house?" Ricky asked, his face looking scared and weak.

"Yeah." I picked myself up and limped toward the yard, walking on the heel of my foot. I left a trail of blood as I went.

I stayed out back while Ricky went in to get Mama. "Oh lands!" she cried, rushing back inside to get a wet washrag. As I plopped down on the back-porch steps, Mr. Lunas appeared from behind the chicken coop, staring at my foot like he'd never seen one before. I scrunched it closer to me, careful not to get blood on my shorts.

Mama came out with a dripping blue rag and wrapped it around my foot, squeezing it tight. She got on her knees and closed her eyes, rocking back and forth, speaking softly. Of course I knew she wasn't praying. She was reciting from the Bible. Ezekiel 16:6. Mama said those were the healing words to stop bleeding. But I was wishing she knew the healing words to stop lockjaw. I kept working my mouth, open and shut, around and around, wondering how long it'd take me to starve to death.

Mama opened her eyes and narrowed them at me. "See what happens when you don't wear shoes!"

"Will I have to get a shot?" I asked, trying not to cry.

"Maybe," she said, the word dragging out of her mouth real slow.

Ricky and Mr. Lunas both leaned forward, watching what was going on. The blue washrag on my foot turned an ugly shade of purple as more and more blood soaked through. Mama started reciting Ezekiel again. Mr. Lunas smiled as he reached out and wiggled my big toe. "You'll be all right." His fingers felt rough, but the wiggle wasn't so bad. Sort of like one of those nursery rhyme wiggles.

"Yeah," Ricky said, acting all smug. "And if you do get a shot, they'll only use a needle about the size of your foot." He held his hands wide apart like he was measuring my foot; then his mouth turned up in a weasel-like grin. "Ouch!"

"Not funny!" I reached my hand out to swat him, but Mama was still rocking and reciting, and I didn't want to accidentally hit her. I decided to take a look at the cut instead.

"Mama, you can stop now. It worked." The cut looked like a pink toothless mouth smiling up at me. The only blood left was on the rag.

"Good," Mama said. "Now let's go to the bath-room and doctor it with Mercurochrome. And don't ever let me catch you trying to hit your brother again."

Sigh.

As soon as Mama finished bandaging my foot, I went out to the back porch and sat down. The clouds were getting thicker and the sky looked like one huge shadow. I could see Ricky out under the shade tree. He was trying to pull the wheels off that junky old baby buggy. He braced his feet against it, jerking on a wheel with the back end of a claw hammer. I kept wondering if it might accidentally slip and hit him in the head, like something out of *The Three Stooges*. It never slipped, but the wheel didn't come off, either. Ricky pulled his foot back and kicked the buggy hard.

Then Mr. Lunas appeared right there beside him, bending down and pointing a finger. I guess he was giving Ricky some suggestions on getting those wheels loose. He reached over and spun the buggy wheel. Not hard, though, just about the speed of a record playing on a hi-fi—a scratchy record with a lot of scrapes and squeaks.

Mr. Lunas held out an oil can.

The wheel turned and turned, and Ricky stared at it. Mr. Lunas was right up next to Ricky's ear, whispering something, I think. Ricky just kept staring at that wheel. I wondered what was so fascinating about it. Everybody had seen wheels turning before. I looked at the spinning wheel too. It turned so fast that you couldn't tell it had spokes—just one solid circle, whirling on its own. Ricky took the oil can and shot a few squirts into the center of the wheel. The scrapes and squeaks mellowed out, but the wheel kept its momentum. We all kept staring at it. Ricky seemed hypnotized, but all that whirling was making me dizzy. Eventually the wheel slowed to a stop, and Mr. Lunas stood up. Then, just like that, Ricky reached over with that hammer and popped that wheel right off the buggy.

"Wooooooooo!" he shouted, holding the wheel up high. I guess oil was the magic potion Ricky hadn't thought of. Mr. Lunas had saved the day. Then a clap of thunder rolled across the sky, shaking the rain out of the clouds. Ricky dropped the wheel, covered his head with his arms, and ran for the porch. Mr. Lunas, with his large belly, waddled in behind him.

"Stop!" I said to Ricky as he shook his hands,

flinging water drops at me. Ricky grinned and rubbed his damp hair.

Mr. Lunas sat down in the chair across from me, looking out toward the field. "This rain is good for the corn," he said.

I looked at the towering stalks, which were turning a copper brown. I heard the chickens fluttering in the coop. The cows gave off a low moo, like they were singing praises in a church choir. The wind picked up and the rain blew in through the screen.

Mr. Lunas nodded. "Yep, this is good for *Earth*."

I suddenly felt prickles as the hairs on the back of my neck stood up. It could have been from the electrical storm, or it could've been the way Mr. Lunas had said the word *Earth*. Like it was a foreign country.

Phase Five—Full Moon

It rained all the next day, so Ricky and I spent most of the time in the cave under the piano. We tossed M&M's at each other, our mouths the target. I got three in a row into Ricky's mouth. When it was his turn he got two into mine, but then he played a trick on me.

"Ready?" he asked, looking like he was concentrating on his aim.

"Ready," I said, stretching my mouth wide open.

But instead of one M&M, Ricky threw a handful. A dozen candy-coated dots flashed in front of my eyes and bounced off my cheeks and chin. "Hey!"

Ricky doubled over laughing. "You should have seen the look on your face!" He couldn't seem to stop laughing. "Your eyes were bigger than drums."

"You didn't fool me, you little twerp," I lied. "I knew you were going to throw a bunch."

"Did not," he said, calming down and hugging his knees.

I started picking up the M&M's we'd dropped. Some were hidden in the creases in my shorts. When I looked back at Ricky, he'd totally changed. He stared out across the room, his face sad, like he'd just lost his best friend.

"What's wrong with you?"

Ricky sighed. "It stinks."

I sniffed the air.

"No, I mean it stinks that I can't go outside."

"It's raining, dummy," I said, seeing the sheets of water washing down the living room windows.

"I know. But I can't go out when it's sunny. I

can't go out when it's rainy. I can't go out when it's cold." He slumped forward and gave me a gloomy look. "I guess I'll be trapped inside for the rest of my life."

Usually I would have sung him my sad song about how *I* couldn't do nothing most of the time because of his skinny little existence, but he looked about as droopy as a wet noodle. I didn't think it'd be smart to get him all agitated. I actually found myself wanting to cheer him up; I just wasn't sure if the right words would spill out. "What would you want to go outside for, anyway? It's muddy and wet and the ground is probably as squishy as oatmeal. I wouldn't want to be out there right now."

"But the barn's dry," he said. "I could build my go-cart in there."

"When it stops raining we'll ask Mama. I'll even help you build it."

He nodded an okay, which surprised the heck out of me because I didn't think he'd want a girl's help. And I doubted I could come up with any practical ideas, like using an oil can. But I nodded back. "Deal."

Then, before I knew what was happening, he flung another handful of M&M's at me. So much for being a sympathetic sister.

☾

Because it was Sunday, Daddy was home, stretched out on the couch watching the Dallas Cowboys play football on TV. An Orange Crush soda bottle sat on the coffee table, wrapped in a cup towel. But if you got close enough, you could smell that it wasn't Orange Crush in the bottle. And every time Daddy took a sip, he'd wipe some foam off his mouth. It's a good thing Mama didn't like football because Daddy would for sure have gotten caught sneaking that beer into the house.

Mr. Lunas paced the floor, back and forth, back and forth. Daddy offered him some pretzels, but he held up his hand, turning them down. I swear if my teeth hadn't been attached to my gums they would have fallen out right then! That was the first time

I'd ever seen Mr. Lunas turn down food! I guess Mama was wrong when she said Mr. Lunas was like an old billy goat and if you turned him loose outside, he'd probably eat all the trash off that flatbed truck.

But he kept pacing, stopping only when Daddy jumped up from the couch to cheer on the Cowboys.

The rain thinned as the day went on. By late afternoon it was just a small drizzle. We had our typical Sunday dinner: fried chicken, creamed potatoes with gravy, and corn on the cob. But we all stayed quiet during the meal, stealing looks at each other. Mr. Lunas sat picking at his food.

"Is everything okay?" Mama asked, looking down at his plate.

"Everything's delicious, Adele," Mr. Lunas answered. "I'm just feeling full these days."

You could say that again! He was looking full, too. If he'd grown a beard and put on a red suit, I bet he could've passed for old Santa himself.

Daddy declared that it was the best meal he'd ever had, then patted his belly and scooted away from the table. I helped Mama clear and wash the dishes. Then we all went outside where it was cool.

A sheer layer of clouds still hung up high, but you could see a few blurry stars here and there. It looked like someone had covered the sky with a giant sheet of wax paper. Just over the house hung a full moon, dim, but managing to shine through. Mama was the first to notice it, and the look on her face became as overcast as the sky. "There's blood around the moon."

I looked up. Sure enough, a small red ring circled it.

"Does that upset you?" Mr. Lunas asked.

Mama brushed her dark curls back from her face. "It's an omen. Something bad is going to happen."

"Oh, Adele!" Daddy said. "You and that superstitious mumbo jumbo."

Mr. Lunas stayed serious. "Why do you think it's a bad omen?"

"It just is. Always has been. I can't name you a time when there was blood around the moon that something bad didn't happen."

Daddy laughed. "Something bad happens all the time. Even when there *ain't* blood around the moon."

He had a point!

Mr. Lunas ignored him and kept looking at Mama. "This bad thing, is it one of your Bible plagues that you saw in the teacup?"

"Could be," Mama said. "The symbol of blood is a harsh one."

"So you're saying that it's the symbol of blood that's bad, right?"

"Of course it is." Mama's voice became low and raspy. "When is blood not a curse? It's red . . . scarlet . . . a wicked, sinful color. When you see a symbol in red, you can bet it's evil."

Mr. Lunas cocked his head. "No disrespect, ma'am, but I took a peek inside that family Bible of yours, and every time Jesus talks, his words are in red. Does that make him evil?"

Mama clammed up and curled her fists into tight balls. She sat as rigid as a pole and just as quiet. Mr. Lunas had certainly called her on that. But what he said got me wondering. Why *does* Jesus talk in red?

The mosquitoes finally figured out where we were, which shortened our visit outside. Daddy said it must rain mosquitoes, too, because they're always worse after a downpour. We all folded up our lawn chairs except Mr. Lunas. "I think I'll stay out here a spell longer," he said. "And like I said, Adele, no disrespect."

Mama huffed as she walked into the house. She headed straight for her bedroom and slammed the door. I went to my room too. I put a record on and leaned back by the window, looking out. Naturally, I was curious as to what foolishness Mr. Lunas was up to tonight. He paced the yard, but instead of walking back and forth like he did in the living room, he marched around in a circle, his hands clasped behind his back. I was sure something was ticking in that brain of his, and I'd have given a whole dollar just to find out what.

Mama banged on my wall after the same record played four times in a row. She always said that drove her nuts, and she just didn't know how anyone could listen to a song over and over and over. Truth was, I wasn't listening. I was thinking about Mr. Lunas and what an oddball he was. I turned the record off and peeked out the window again. The moon was pretty high now and giving off a decent amount of light. I could see Mr. Lunas near the cornfield, holding a coffee can. Buddy wagged along with him.

I was suddenly as curious as a bystander at a train wreck. I just couldn't help it. I had to know what Mr. Lunas was doing out there. Buddy saw me coming out and ran to meet me. I wandered over to Mr. Lunas, who'd set the coffee can down on the ground.

"What're you doing?" I asked.

"Making moonshine," he said, rubbing his chin.

I stood there, stunned for a second. "You're making homemade whiskey?"

Mr. Lunas let a laugh roll out from that big belly of his. "No. Nothing illegal."

"Then what have you got in there?"

He looked at me and grinned. "Moonbeams."

I leaned forward and peeped in, expecting to see tiny lights fluttering around like the fireflies winking in the pasture. But all I saw was a can full of water, my shadow making the liquid look dark and inky. "That's bullcorn. I don't see any moonbeams."

Mr. Lunas moved the can back into the moonlight. "You can't see them because the water is soaking them up."

"Why would you want to have moonbeam-soaked water?" I asked. It was the craziest notion I'd ever heard.

"Why would you want gasoline for your car?"

I shook my head to show him what a dumb question that was. "It can't go nowhere without gas."

Mr. Lunas gave me one of those big, luminous

smiles of his. His grins seemed to have gotten bigger along with his body. "Precisely," he said.

"Are you going somewhere?"

He tilted his round gray head and sighed. "Eventually."

I wouldn't let up. "Where?"

I could see he was weary of my questions, but I was weary too. Not so much of him as of all this weirdness about him. He'd been here a couple of weeks, living in our house—okay, outside our house—and eating our food. So why was he still such a stranger?

"Where I fit in best," he replied.

I couldn't imagine where that'd be.

"Have a sip," he said, offering the coffee can to me.

I took a quick step back, then mustered up the nerve to peek in. It was hard to tell in the dark if it was nothing but water and moonbeams. The surface looked like a transparent shadow. I'd seen Mama put tea bags in a big jug of water and set it out in the sun to make tea, but I'd never seen anybody make tea out of moonbeams before. Carefully taking the can, I leaned closer and sniffed. Smelled like water . . . or what I thought water smelled like. I took a tiny sip.

"Whaddya think?" Mr. Lunas asked.

"Tastes like water. Just water."

He smiled. "It is water."

"But shouldn't the moonbeams taste like something?"

Mr. Lunas took the can and swished the water around some more. "What do you think moonbeams should taste like?"

I shrugged. "How the heck should I know? Marshmallows?"

"Take another sip," he said, offering it to me again. "A bigger sip."

I did. Then I took another, and another, and then a big gulp. I'll be durned if it didn't taste a little like marshmallows!

"See?" he said, turning the can around and taking a swig from the other side. "Some of the best treats are the simple ones."

"Everything around here is simple. Simple is just about all we know."

He offered the coffee can to me again. "Well, who wants to know complex?"

I did. At least just a taste of it, anyway. It could be as sweet as this moonshine.

Mr. Lunas might have been collecting moonbeams, but I was collecting a swarm of mosquitoes and biting flies. And I was plumb tired of scratching. I said goodnight and headed back up to the house. As I got inside, I could hear Mama and Daddy going at it again.

"He's been here for two weeks!" Mama said, her voice muffled by the walls.

"Adele, I can't throw him out! He's our company. He saved my life, remember?"

"I'm tired of him being stuck around this house all day, wandering in and out. He's been eating us out of house and home, which isn't hard to do since you don't have a job and we can barely buy groceries anyway! He's as worthless as you are. And don't think you can fool me anymore, either. I've been smelling beer on your breath—"

I'd heard enough. I went to my room and got ready for bed. Their argument still seeped through the walls, so I grabbed my pillow and squeezed it over my ears. I kept my light off and sat looking out the window.

There were Mr. Lunas and Buddy, wandering out near the cornfield. I watched Mr. Lunas pick up the coffee can, swirl the water around, then turn it up for a long drink. I could almost taste the marshmallow as I watched him gulp that whole thing down.

I settled back onto the bed. Could Mama really talk Daddy into kicking Mr. Lunas out of the house? I hoped not. He was the one thing that made this summer different from all the others. Different? Yeah. Different was good. Suddenly I stopped thinking and froze on the spot. I heard Buddy out near the cornfield . . . howling at the moon again.

Phase Six—Waning Gibbous

M r. Lunas made himself scarce. We barely saw him during the next couple of days. I wondered if he'd heard Mama and Daddy fighting. Or maybe he just knew something was up because they weren't speaking to each other. I hated that.

Mr. Lunas was a lot like a puzzle. Trying to figure him out took my mind off the blues and the blahs. But now he would leave before breakfast and come back after dinner each day. He'd lost a few pounds, and his jolly face was looking thinner.

Daddy sliced open a watermelon for dessert one night, and Mr. Lunas just sat and nodded while we spit out seeds and dribbled juice down our chins. I couldn't imagine anybody turning down watermelon!

I guess he was still drinking that moon water, although the moon was starting to get a dark rim around its edges. It was a pretty sight, sitting out at night and watching it shine down on the cornfield, but the face on the moon was disappearing, a little at a time.

"I finally got the wheels off that baby buggy," Ricky said as we sat on the porch one morning, watching fat cotton clouds breeze across the sky.

"It took you long enough." I could see some scrapes and small cuts on his hands. I guess that oil can didn't work quite as well as when Mr. Lunas was there. Or maybe Ricky couldn't spin the wheels as good. "Wait a minute!" I said, remembering something. "How did you get the wheels off? You haven't even been outside." Mama had been in such a bad mood the last two days that

Ricky hadn't dared ask to go out. When Mama was in a mood she could snap like a crocodile.

Ricky grinned and put his finger over his lips.

"That's bullcorn! You haven't been sneaking out, have you?"

He nodded.

"Sneaking out?"

"Shhh! Don't go telling the whole world, idiot!"

I couldn't believe that baby Ricky, Mama's little pet, would disobey her. But knowing it sure brought out the devil in me. "You know, if you get caught they may lock you in your room for eternity . . . or longer!"

"I won't get caught."

"Are you sure?" I waggled my eyebrows at him to show that I had some leverage.

"You better not tell!" Ricky's face was starting to turn a few shades of purple, like a spring turnip.

"What'll you give me not to?"

"It's what I'll give you if you *do* tell that you need to worry about." He spouted the words like a bully, but his skinny little butt didn't scare me none. It was his anxious look that made me cow down.

"Janine, I've got to finish that go-cart." I could hear a hint of begging in his voice. "It sure ain't gonna build itself, and it's all I can think about. Heck, it's already August. I want a chance to ride it down the hill before school starts, 'cause you know darn well Mama won't let me go outside after school. And the whole rest of the day is swallowed up at school."

It was true. Mama only let Ricky outside to ride the bus to school and then home. She always went on and on in the mornings about whether he was too sick to attend or not, and in the afternoons she put him straight to bed, no matter how he felt. Of course she shipped me off every day, no matter what kind of bellyache I complained about. She'd even sent a permanent note to Ricky's teacher saying he wasn't allowed to go out for recess. I overheard his teacher once telling another teacher that it was a miserable existence. I'm just thankful that

God put my gizzard in right. At least I can go out at recess, even with a bellyache.

"So what are you planning to do?" I asked him.

We could hear Mama off in the kitchen, baking pies. She had the radio on, and Hank Williams was whining about somebody's cheating heart. We could hear Mama singing along with him.

"She seems to be in a good mood today," Ricky said.

"I guess because Mr. Lunas hasn't been around much."

Ricky slumped when I said that. He seemed to like Mr. Lunas about as much as Buddy did. And I have to admit, as odd as he was, I liked him too.

"You think I should ask Mama if I can go out today?" Ricky wondered.

"I don't know. She could say yes because she sounds happy. Or she could get mad and say no and be in a bad mood again."

Ricky shrugged. "Would you ask her?"

"Me? It's your dumb go-cart."

"Yeah, but you promised to help me build it."

79

"I was just doing my sisterly duty and trying to cheer you up. And I already sliced a chunk out of my foot on that thing." I looked down at the wound, now barely visible. It reminded me of something, but I couldn't quite figure out what. A crooked grin? A quarter moon? I was just thankful it healed so fast that I didn't get lockjaw.

"I'll let you go down the hill in it if you ask her." He looked at me with puppy-dog eyes.

"I'll go down the hill in it anyway."

"How?" Ricky asked, scrunching his eyebrows.

"I'll just ride it after school."

I might as well have picked up a stick and beat the tar out of him. He suddenly looked whupped. "You're hateful. I wish it was you who was stuck inside all the time instead of me!"

"I *am* stuck inside all the time."

"Liar," he said, his face taking on that turnip color again. "You can go outside anytime you want."

True as that was, I couldn't think of many reasons I even wanted to go outside. Not by myself, anyway. Then I thought about what Ricky's teacher had said. I had to agree, it really must be a miserable existence. "Fine. I won't ride your dumb go-cart after school."

His face clouded up and I was afraid he might cry. "There won't be a go-cart to ride after school if I can't go outside to build it."

I couldn't argue with that, plus I was getting tired of feeling like a bully. "Okay, okay! I'll ask her."

We tiptoed inside and Ricky stood next to the kitchen door, out of sight. I saw Mama, rolling out a piecrust, her hands as white as the morning clouds. She scratched her nose with her forearm since her hands were covered in flour, and her big bottom wiggled to the music playing on the radio.

"Mama," I said, low and sweet. "I was wondering something."

Mama's behind stopped wiggling, but she kept rolling the dough. "What're you wondering about?"

"Well . . . I . . . I . . ." I felt like I needed

someone to slap me on the back and knock the words out of my mouth.

"Stop stuttering and tell me," Mama said. She didn't sound mad. That was good.

"I was wondering if Ricky could go outside with me today."

Mama flipped the piecrust over and a big puff of flour dust flew up around it. "Can't y'all play in the house? It's too darn hot for Ricky to go outside."

I wasn't sure how to argue with that. Mama had a portable fan pointing at her from the top of the icebox, but she was still sweating. There were wet rings on her dress, under her armpits, and around her collar.

"We could play under the shade tree."

"I bet it's a hundred degrees in that shade."

She was probably right. "Maybe we could stretch an extension cord outside and put a fan under the tree to blow on us."

Mama gave me a stern look. "You know darn well that Ricky can't have that wind blowing down his lungs."

"But that's bullcorn!" Oops! I'd done it again.

"Don't you start shooting your mouth off at me, young lady!" She pointed her sticky white finger in my face. Stringy bits of dough hung from it. Then she walked to the kitchen door and waggled her finger on the other side of it. "And you listen to me, mister! You need to start thinking more about your health. You know Daddy and I do the best we can for you. Now, you two go play somewhere in the house. I've got pies to put in the oven, and I want to get it done before the afternoon heat sets in and makes this kitchen too unbearable."

I didn't have to look at Ricky's face. We both knew when Mama had the final word.

Ricky stomped through the kitchen door and headed for the living room. I figured he was planning to sulk inside the cave. I followed him and crawled under.

"I should run away from home," he said, his voice cracking and his eyes watery.

"Then you'll never get your go-cart built."

He nodded his head hard. "Yeah, I will. I'm going to build my go-cart anyway. Then I'll run away in it!"

That sounded plumb stupid. "Unless you plan to put a motor on it, you'll have to run away downhill."

Ricky hugged his legs and laid his head on his knees. "Maybe I'll find an old lawn mower motor to put on it."

"Or maybe you can sprinkle moondust on it and sail across the sky," a voice said from across the living room.

Ricky and I both peeked through the piano bench. There was Mr. Lunas, sitting in a chair by the front door. He looked smaller perching there, his head resting on his hand.

"You're dreaming," Ricky said as he curled back into a ball to pout.

"And so are you," Mr. Lunas replied. He got up from the chair and slowly crept across the room. His walk was starting to look weak, like when we'd first met him. As he went by the piano, he bent down and smiled. "But it's good to dream, Ricky. It's good."

I watched him shuffle by, wondering what *he* dreamed about. Did old folks still have dreams?

"It's more than a dream," Ricky whispered to me. "It's my only chance. I can either rot in this house or I can zoom out of here."

I didn't whisper anything back. Mostly because I thought he was dreaming too. And he wasn't the only one rotting in this house. We were all starting to smell overripe.

We didn't stay in the cave that afternoon, and we didn't play in Ricky's room, either. I spent the afternoon listening to records and laying on the bed, reading *Mr. Popper's Penguins*. Here I sat, in Texas, the oven of America, while Mr. Popper had a wild time with his flapping friends from the Antarctic. I looked up for a minute to rest my eyes and saw Mr. Lunas coming out of the chicken coop. He had an ear of corn in one hand and an egg in the other. Maybe that was why he wasn't eating anymore. Maybe he was sneaking off somewhere and making his own corn fritters. Naw . . . that was bullcorn. Why would he do that? Unless he was worried about us not having enough food. I watched him lay the corn and the egg down next to the coffee can, then shoo Buddy away from them. He had one of Mama's towels from the kitchen, and he used it to cover them up.

I decided to play Nancy Drew and see if I could solve the mystery of Mr. Lunas. I hurried outside before he could wander off.

"Whatcha got?" I asked him, pointing at the things hidden under the towel.

"Art supplies," he answered.

Why did I know he'd make a puzzle out of it? Maybe I should have stayed in my room after all. But like Nancy Drew, I pressed on. "Are you going to paint a picture?"

Buddy rolled the egg out with his snout, and Mr. Lunas rolled it right back. "Well, I'm not exactly Michelangelo," he said, covering the corn and the egg with the towel again.

"Michelangelo? Who's he?"

"An artist."

I looked at the hidden objects again, wondering what Nancy Drew would ask next. "Hmmm . . . did he use corn and eggs to paint his pictures?"

Mr. Lunas tilted his head at me. "He used his imagination."

"But using your imagination is only painting pictures in your head."

"Yes!" he said, sounding like I'd discovered gold. "Isn't that where all pictures start?"

Why did every conversation with him have to be a riddle? "Mr. Lunas, you're teasing me."

He ruffled my hair with his hand. "I am, aren't I?"

"Well, aren't you going to give me a straight answer?"

He grinned a mile-wide grin. "But that wouldn't be teasing then, would it?"

"Mr. Lunas!"

He tilted his old gray head again. "I've given you nothing but straight answers, Janine. In time you'll know how to line them up."

He shuffled away, Buddy hard on his heels. Why was this so much easier for Nancy Drew?

C

I was trying to cool off on the back porch when Daddy's Chevy puttered in. He stopped to pet Buddy, then walked up the driveway with his hand behind his back.

I couldn't help smiling. "What're you hiding?"

Daddy smiled right back. "Something for my special girl."

I jumped at his sleeve and tried to wrestle his arm around to the front.

"Not for you, silly thing. It's for your mother."

I dropped my arms and backed away. What a mean trick! As he went inside, I saw a bunch of daisies in his fist, all tied up in a big yellow bow.

In all my life, I'd never seen Daddy bring Mama flowers. Not on her birthday, or Mother's Day, or even their anniversary. Daddy liked to buy her chocolates instead. Something must be up!

I rushed in after him, letting the screen door

slam. Mama was getting the dinner plates down. Daddy popped the flowers out from behind him and stretched his hand out, grinning hard. Mama just stood there, looking like she'd never seen flowers before.

"What're those for?"

"I might have a job!" he said, the words shooting out like a bottle rocket.

"Really?" Mama clapped her hands together. She rushed forward and threw her arms around Daddy's neck, almost crushing the daisies. She giggled real silly as she took out a jar to use as a vase. "Where at?" she asked.

"Red Johnson is building a new warehouse for his moving business. It's almost complete. Now he's hiring folks to run it. I won't find out for sure until next week, but I might end up as manager."

Mama still hung on to that cabinet door, her eyes fixed on Daddy. "Why next week?"

"His cousin George may be moving here from Amarillo. If he does, Red will give the manager position to him."

Mama slammed the cabinet door. "Red's one of your closest friends. Surely he'll give you the job."

"But George is his cousin. And anyway, he probably won't take it. His wife grew up in Amarillo and says she ain't moving to save her life."

Mama let out a sigh. "Well, let's keep our fingers crossed that she wears the pants in the family."

Daddy laughed and went over to give her another hug. "Don't worry, Adele. Everything will work out."

Ricky walked in, dragging his feet. Mama and Daddy looked at him real strange, like he had four heads and scales. "What's wrong, baby?" Mama said, rushing over to feel his forehead.

Ricky swooned, and blood started dripping from his nose. Daddy picked him up and rushed into the living room. He gently laid Ricky down on the couch. Mama came in with a towel and a glass of water. "I'll bet you're just too hot," she said, wiping his nose and tilting the glass to his mouth. He barely drank. It looked like his throat didn't know how to swallow. "Go put him to bed," Mama said.

As Daddy scooped him up again, Ricky looked toward me with droopy, glassy eyes. His mouth opened a little, and with some effort, he whispered, "Janine."

Phase Seven—Last Quarter

Ricky dangled like a puppet as Daddy laid him down on the bed. He could barely keep his eyes open, and his breathing was hard and rough. No wonder. His room was so hot, it felt like all the air had been sucked out of it. Even I had trouble taking a breath. If only Mama would turn on a fan.

"I'll drive down to the pay phone and call the doctor," Daddy said, fishing his keys out of his pants pocket.

Mama didn't say a word, but the look in her

eyes pleaded "Hurry." She brushed the hair off Ricky's forehead. It was so thick with sweat, she had to pick some of it loose with her fingers. "Go get me a wet washrag, Janine."

I didn't waste a second. I ran to the bathroom and grabbed one of the blue washcloths. Ricky liked blue. I didn't wring it out very well, and it dripped all the way back to his room. I thought Mama would lay it on his forehead, but she put the washrag on his mouth instead, pushing a little of it inside. She smiled down at him. "Maybe this will keep you from being so thirsty." She squeezed the rag a little so water could drip into his mouth. "It's just like when you were a baby. I used to fill a washrag with butter and sugar. You'd suck all that sweet cream out and lay there with that rag in your mouth until you fell asleep."

Until he was five years old, Ricky would lay on the couch, sucking on a washcloth and watching cartoons. I never understood then why he'd want an old washrag in his mouth. And I couldn't stand here and watch it now, either.

I went out on the back porch, where the air smelled as sweet as a melon. The sun was low in the sky. I stood there, looking out at the pasture, hearing the cows crying to be milked. The chickens squawked and fluttered, and then I saw Mr. Lunas coming out of the chicken coop. He was holding two eggs and heading toward the cornfield. Buddy followed. I ran out to him.

"Ricky's real sick."

"What?" Mr. Lunas said, placing the eggs in the same coffee can he'd used to make moon water.

"He's real sick. Real, real sick! Daddy went to call the doctor."

He gazed at me, a pained look on his face. "Is there anything I can do?"

"I hope so," I egged. "You said you were in the medical corps in the service—"

He held up his hand to stop me before more words came spilling out my mouth.

"That was a long time ago. And even then I only did some patching up . . . like your mother did for your foot."

95

"Can you try?" I was working to keep my voice steady, but he had to hear how scared I was.

"Let's see how he is in a couple of days, okay?"

A couple of days! Why not now?

He crouched down and covered the coffee can with the towel. I've never seen anyone put so much effort into such a tiny task. Then I got a good look at him. In just a few days' time, Mr. Lunas looked like he'd lost a hundred pounds. His face was shadowed and wrinkled, and he moved with about as much power as a snail. A snail in pain.

"Are you okay?" I asked him.

He gave me a half grin. "Just my rheumatism," he said.

Feeling awkward, I reached down and rubbed Buddy's neck. "I better get back in case they need me." I couldn't imagine why they'd need me, but just in case.

I hurried back, slipping into the kitchen. The house felt like a tomb. So did the air. Everything was dead quiet, except for the rumbling in my stomach. It reminded me that we'd skipped dinner. I plopped some chicken and dumplings on a plate and sat down all alone. With my stomach in jitters, all I wanted was a few bites. I didn't even get those down before Daddy came busting through the back door. I ran down the hall to hear what had happened.

"Dr. Littlefield said to give Ricky an extra dose of the medicine, and that he'll be out in the morning to look him over," Daddy said.

Mama shushed him and pointed to Ricky. I had to look twice to make sure he was just sleeping. His face was the color of the ashes in Daddy's barbecue pit, but the dark circles under his eyes were more like the charcoal. I imagined that this was just what a dead person looked like, but I shooed that thought away quick! Not Ricky. He might be a little pain in the butt, but he was still my baby brother. Those bites of chicken and dumpling threatened to come up. Guilt overtook my fear, and I got to thinking that maybe my life wouldn't be so great if Ricky were gone.

Mama sat down next to him, mumbling. I knew it was more of those healing passages from the Bible. I guess she knew one for every ailment there was. I went back to the kitchen and that wasted plate of chicken and dumplings. And the hope that Mama's Bible verses would serve as the extra dose of medicine Ricky needed.

The next morning I heard voices drifting down the hall. I peeked in to see Mama, Daddy, Mr. Lunas, and Dr. Littlefield sitting at the kitchen table, drinking coffee.

Dr. Littlefield's face was as stern as a statue. "I'm telling you, Adele, there's no guarantee that surgery would help. Now, let's just keep him on this medicine and see how he does. We've had these close calls before."

Mama's eyes were red from tears. "We've tried every medicine there is! He still has the cough, and the nosebleeds, and some days I think a breeze is going to come along and blow him away. He never gains an ounce. And his heart . . ." She sobbed into her hands. "I can't lose my baby! I just can't!"

Daddy put his arm around Mama, but she pushed him away. I couldn't help looking at the jar of daisies on top of the icebox. They were the only cheerful thing in the room. I kept thinking that the doctor had to be right. The medicine would work. Ricky would be okay.

Mr. Lunas excused himself from the table and headed toward Ricky's room. "Where are you going?" Mama yelled, glaring at him like she had the first evening he came out of the cornfield.

"I thought I'd just look in on him."

Mama's red eyes turned scarlet and lit with fire. "Stay out! I don't want nobody disturbing him."

"Calm down," Daddy said, nearly whispering.

"Calm down! My baby's lying in that room, barely alive, and you're telling me to calm down? Like you've got room to talk. You're the reason we're in this mess in the first place. Maybe if you had a job we could afford some decent health care.

And what about him?" She pointed an angry finger at Mr. Lunas. "How do we know he didn't bring in some foreign germ? Not to mention him being an extra mouth to feed?"

That wasn't rightly true anymore. I hadn't seen Mr. Lunas eat anything in days.

Mr. Lunas held up a hand and turned toward the back door. "I'll just step out for a while."

I couldn't help being embarrassed. Even in an emergency, it's plumb wrong to say hateful things like that to a person's face. Especially a harmless old man like Mr. Lunas. But I'm sure he knew that Mama was just feeling helpless and talking out the top of her head.

I'd had enough and went back to my room while Dr. Littlefield and Daddy were trying to get Mama under control. I locked myself away, not really sure what to do. I couldn't play my records because Mama would surely have a fit about the noise. I didn't have Ricky to play with, and Buddy just hung around Mr. Lunas these days. He'd stopped being our dog weeks ago. I laid on the bed and stared at the wallpaper. I stared hard. So hard, I looked right past it. I looked at a time in the future when I was grown up, living in Hollywood with a mansion and servants. I'd pick up the phone and call Italy or France. "Yes, this is Janine calling from Hollywood. Would you please send over your best doctors? The ones that specialize in gizzards." Then Ricky would be cured, and I would give him a part in my next movie. Or even better, I'd grow up to be a doctor myself. Girls can be doctors. I know because I've seen Dr. Joyce Brothers on TV. And I wouldn't just cure Ricky, I'd cure everyone I touched. Life would be perfect.

I laid around, dozing and daydreaming most of the morning. When I went back into the kitchen, it was empty. I made a peanut butter sandwich and ducked into the cave to eat it. It wasn't the same, without Ricky. I closed my eyes and prayed. It'd be a real long time before I grew up to become a doctor, and Ricky needed help now. There had to be something I could do.

Mama wouldn't let anyone in Ricky's room. She fussed that folks being in there would just upset him. She was the only one allowed, and she stayed there all the time. She only came out to go to the bathroom or wet a rag. Daddy made soup, but Mama wouldn't allow him in with it. She took the bowl from him at the door and closed it.

"He's my son, too," Daddy said as the door shut in his face. He sat at the table, his head in his hands. I sat down next to him. He rubbed his face so hard I thought he'd rub it right off. When he looked at me, his eyebrows were bushy and wild. A gentle smile crept across his face, which, under the circumstances, didn't seem natural. Then he said, "Hey, pumpkin. You want a Popsicle?"

At first I wasn't sure what he meant. There were no Popsicles in the freezer. He stood up, and I heard his car keys jingling in his hand.

"Okay!"

It'd been a while since I'd sat in the front seat

of Daddy's car. The vinyl had a giant rip in it that curled up, and it scratched my leg. I tried to adjust the stuffing inside to cover it, but it wasn't working. I finally ignored it, just happy to be going somewhere at last.

Daddy backed out of the driveway, the Chevy's tires crunching on the gravel. The old car sputtered for a minute; then, with a jolt, it picked up speed, and we sailed down the road. I stuck my head out the window to feel the wind on my face. It cooled my cheeks and whistled in my ears. The radio was set to the hillbilly station, but Daddy patted my knee and said, "You can change the channel if you want."

I slowly turned the knob, listening to broken voices and crackling static. I stopped when I heard Chubby Checker inviting me to do "The Twist."

Going to the 7-Eleven was like going to another town. It's the closest store to our house, but it still took about twenty minutes to get there. I didn't mind. After being stuck at home all summer, this was like going on vacation.

Daddy paid for two Popsicles, and we sat in the car, licking the red juice that melted down the sides. A group of kids sat on the ground out front, drinking sodas and laughing. They all looked a few years older than me, but I couldn't help wishing I had a crowd of friends like that to hang out with at the 7-Eleven. One boy was even chugging a beer, though he didn't look nearly old enough to have it. I figured he must be a show-off, since they were all cheering him on. I could only hear small chunks of their conversations, but it was enough to know that their summer didn't involve sick brothers and strange houseguests. And their laughter made me plumb jealous.

Daddy was awful quiet. I could tell he was itching to say something, so I decided to break the silence and get him started. "This is good." I slid the whole Popsicle in my mouth, chilling my tongue.

He didn't even look at me. He just gazed at his Popsicle and nodded his head. "Janine, I wanted you to know that things aren't going too good right now."

Like I didn't already know that! But I didn't let on that I did. "Why?" I asked, thinking he'd talk about Ricky being so sick.

"We don't have any money, and . . . well . . . it looks like we might have to pay for a funeral real soon."

Those words crashed into me, making my Popsicle drop out of my hand and onto my lap. "No." I shook my head. "You're going to get a job. Ricky's going to get better. He's even going to build his go-cart. I'm going to help him. He already has the lumber!"

Daddy crossed his arms on the steering wheel and leaned his head on it. "I might be using that lumber to build a coffin." His voice cracked and hitched, and a puddle of tears came pouring out of his eyes. I was tongue-tied, not knowing what to say or do. I realized then that daddies cry too.

The tears that had been dammed up inside me broke loose, and I squalled along with him. "He's gonna get better, Daddy. I promise." It was all I could think to say, even though I knew it was a sin to break a promise.

Daddy wiped his eyes and nose on his sleeve and sat up. He tossed the rest of his Popsicle out the window and cleared his throat. "I just wanted you to know how things were." He started the engine and backed out of the 7-Eleven parking lot. The lively lit store got smaller and smaller, and soon we were back on the road to the middle of nowhere—home.

I cried myself to sleep that night and dreamed that Mr. Lunas was building a coffin in the backyard. I woke up to the sound of movement outside the window. It was Buddy. He was laying in the dirt beside the house. "Good boy," I said, patting on the window screen.

He looked up in the dark, his brown eyes drooping. Everyone was sad, even Buddy. I thought about dogs being smarter than humans and figured he must know about Ricky too. I flinched when I caught a glimpse of Mr. Lunas leaning against a tree not too far from my window. He looked more like a rail propped against it, and I wondered if his gizzard was in backwards too. I don't think he saw me, because he was too busy staring off at a half-moon, barely risen in the sky.

I went to Ricky's bedroom and put my ear to the door. It was quiet. I wanted to peek in. I hadn't seen him in two days, and I missed him something fierce. I needed to see him sitting up, laughing and joking. I turned the knob in slow motion and opened the door without making the least bit of noise. The minute I stuck my head in, the hot air clutched me like a fist. The room smelled of blood and vomit. I had to back away quick and catch my breath. Then it hit me: Ricky was alone. All alone. Where was Mama?

I stuck my head in again, and this time I wasn't so quiet about it. I walked over to the bed and looked down. Ricky was just a glob of jelly, piled on top of the sheets. His pajamas were soaked from sweat, and his skin was as slick and white as one of my porcelain dolls.

When I sat down next to him, he opened his eyes. His lids fluttered; then a teeny crease of a smile appeared. "You came to see me."

"I wanted to come sooner, but you know Mama."

I thought he nodded, but it was hard to tell. He had no strength at all.

"Janine," he said, his voice sounding like an old man's. "Looks like I'm going to die."

"That's bullcorn! Stop that dumb talk."

"It's okay," he continued. "I'm not scared. Probably 'cause I'm too tired to be scared. Everything hurts. Even when I talk."

"Then don't talk. Problem is, you just don't feel good right now." I tried to sound courageous, hoping it would rub off on him. "You'll feel great in a day or two. Then you'll build your go-cart and go sailing down the hill."

His eyes rolled over dark. "Yeah. I really wanted to ride that go-cart."

"You will," I said. I tried to put as much meaning behind it as I could, but another minute in this stinking hot room, I thought even I might die.

He laid there, quiet, then strained to raise his head and look at me. "I'll miss you something awful."

Those words opened the floodgates again. Tears poured out of me like rain from the sky. "I'll miss you too . . . even more."

I hugged him close, his body clammy and cool, even in that heat. I could feel his heart beating against me, and I prayed it wouldn't stop. I just held him tight, not caring if Mama came in and caught me. Not caring if she gave me the switching of my life. Not caring about anything but holding my little brother next to me. And no matter what, I wasn't ever going to let him go.

Phase Eight—Waning Crescent

hen I woke up the next morning the house felt empty, and so did I. My eyes were just puffy pink bubbles from crying the night before. They ached and burned, and I rubbed them hard with my fists. I heard the rooster crow, then Daddy snore, and I looked out the window at the smears of cotton-candy clouds. It was a lot earlier than my usual wake-up time. Mr. Lunas was curled up on a lawn chair out back. He was shrinking each day and starting to look more like the old scarecrow he'd been that first evening I met him. But why? Why had he stopped eating? Maybe later I'd take some buttered toast out to him for breakfast. His withering got me to thinking about Ricky . . . Ricky! That empty feeling inside me began to fill up.

It started with a trembling in my hands, then it moved to my arms, then my shoulders. It sprouted through my body like a wild dewberry vine. Before I knew it, I was ready to scream. But instead, I dug in my closet and pulled out my old tennis shoes. I hadn't worn shoes since the last day of school, and it seemed my feet had grown some. I tugged them on anyway. The volcano kept rising inside me as I went outside. The morning air hung soft as a thistle, and there were some patches of dew on the ground. I didn't care. Buddy came up, thinking I would feed him. I didn't. Instead, I ran.

My feet were the only thing in control as I raced past Mr. Lunas and the cornfield. Buddy ran too. I glided by the barn and through the pasture, jumping rocks, bull nettles, and cow patties. I circled the old flatbed truck, scaring a small green snake that slithered under one of the rusty tire rims. The volcano had erupted, and nothing could stop it. My legs burned, but I kept running. There was a stitch in my side and I gasped for air, but I kept going. I had to run. I couldn't stop. I needed to burn off everything that had swollen inside me during this long, hot summer vacation.

I imagined Ricky running beside me, grinning and yelling, "Race ya!" And I wouldn't've said a word about letting him win. I came back around the barn and ran straight for the old shade tree. Buddy dashed in front, almost tripping me. We stopped and panted, gasping for breath. I hugged the tree just to hold myself up. When I wiped the sweat from my eyes, I saw something that really made that volcano sizzle. Lying there in the shade, like pieces of a puzzle, were lumber, nails, bolts, and buggy wheels. All laid out like a go-cart.

I had never understood how Ricky had imagined that go-cart before. But seeing it now, pieced together on the ground, it made perfect sense. At that moment, I knew what I had to do.

I tried to sneak back into the house for a bowl of cereal and a glass of milk, but when I went into the kitchen, there sat Mama and Mr. Lunas. Mama looked like an old rag that had been wrung out and left in the sun to dry. Her face had new lines and shadows that hadn't been there before. Mr. Lunas didn't look much better. The whole room was a box of gloom. I couldn't tell whether or not Mama had apologized to Mr. Lunas for those nasty things she'd said about him, but being a good Christian woman, I was guessing she'd done the right thing. I didn't see Daddy anywhere and figured he must be sitting with Ricky.

"Where've you been?" she asked me, her voice a raspy whisper.

"Playing with Buddy." Oops! I wished I'd made up a different lie. Mama probably thought I was the worst sister in the whole world. My brother's laying in his bed, dying of Backward-Gizzard Disease, and now she'd think I was out playing instead of grieving.

"Did you feed him?" she asked.

"I'll do it," Mr. Lunas said. He scooted away from the table and hobbled to the sink. His pants were bagging again and his belt was pulled so tight, the end of it hung down in front. He bent over and opened the cabinet where Mama kept the dog food. I couldn't help wondering if he'd ever manage to straighten himself back up. But he did . . . s-l-o-w-l-y.

I hurried over and closed the cabinet door for him. He gave me a wink as he walked away, dog food in hand. I got my favorite cereal and bowl. When I finally sat at the table, Mama gave me the look of doom.

"How's Ricky?" I managed to ask.

"Not much different than last night when you were in his room."

My face burned from fear. I had to say something fast. I couldn't think of anything that didn't involve spreading germs, so I decided to tell the truth. "I couldn't help it, Mama. I missed him."

Mama hung her head and sobbed. "I don't guess it's gonna make much difference now anyway. He should be in a hospital where the air is sterile and clean, not this old run-down house with holes in the roof and cracks in the—"

I think she was crying, but her eyes were dry. She surely must have run out of tears by now. I finished my breakfast and stood up to clear the dishes. "I'll be out by the old shade tree."

She just kept her head resting on her hand and never said a word.

☾

Buddy joined me out there, his tongue and tail both wagging away. I patted his head, then circled the layout of the go-cart. I could see how it was meant to be put together, but I didn't know squat about nuts and bolts. I did know how to pound a hammer, though, so that's exactly what I did.

I nailed the long board to the thick shorter ones just the way Ricky had placed them. I hammered hard, missing a few times and putting round dents in the wood. Even though the shade tree was a good distance from the house, I couldn't help worrying that Daddy might come out and fuss about the noise disturbing Ricky. I didn't want to get caught.

When I first tried hammering the nail into the end board, it bent right in half. It took me five minutes and most of my strength to tug it out. My second try got it in straight as a pencil. I stood back to see how it looked. Not as even as I'd have liked, but it should work. I tilted my head, thinking the boards looked a lot like a giant letter "I." I squatted down again, ready to tackle the wheels. That's when the screen door slammed and Daddy came stomping down the back steps, flinging his arms like a wild man and screaming at the top of his lungs. "He's my son too! Remember? He's my son, too!"

Daddy ran toward one of the lawn chairs and kicked it hard. It flew up into the air, then landed with a bang, bending the aluminum arm on one side. Some dirty words flew out of his mouth as he picked up the warped lawn chair and bashed it against the chicken coop. The chickens squawked and fluttered like crazy, their feathers flying all over the place.

I suddenly got scared that he'd come over and destroy what little work I'd done on the go-cart, so I headed him off, just walking up like nothing was going on, crossing my arms when I got close to him. "What's wrong, Daddy?"

"Your danged mama, that's what's wrong! The woman's gone plain nuts. All I did was tell her to take a nice bubble bath and have a nap. That I'd look out for Ricky today. She went plumb crazy. Told me that I wasn't going to keep her away from her little boy, then she shoved me clean out of the room. When I thought she'd calmed down I tried to go back in, but she'd moved the dresser in front of the door to keep me out. This business has made her plain loco!" He kicked the ground, stirring up dirt.

"Can't we just take Ricky to the hospital like Mama wants?"

Daddy laughed like I'd told the funniest joke he'd ever heard, but he looked like he might cry at the same time. "I wish it was that simple, Janine. We ain't got money for a hospital. We ain't got insurance. And the charity hospital, why, they'd just let him die." Daddy looked down at the ground and whispered, "He can do that here."

I felt my blood draining at those words and I ran up, wrapping myself around Daddy's waist. I held tight. "He ain't gonna die, Daddy. He ain't!"

He hugged me close, but even his strong arms couldn't shelter me from that awful word. I hated that word! Maybe Ricky wouldn't die if people would just stop talking about it. I buried my face in Daddy's shirt, which smelled like a mixture of Tide detergent, Old Spice, and sweat. I clung to him and that smell, remembering how he could always make things better when I was sad. He loosened my grip.

"We've got to be strong for Mama," he said, looking straight down at me. "If she's acting like this now . . . well . . . no telling what she'll be like when the worst comes."

I felt like butter that had been left out in the

sun. I walked away without saying another word. I went straight to the living room and crawled into the cave. Curling up, I thought about the world and how unfair it was. The way the grown-ups were talking, finishing that go-cart would just be a big waste of time. But the more I thought about it, the more important it became. I was going to do what I had to for Ricky. And I knew I had to do it quick.

☾

I raced back outside to the shade tree, where I hammered and worked for a whole hour. And when I finished, I had something that resembled a go-cart, even if it was still just a big old letter "I" with wheels.

"That's a mighty fine piece of transportation you've got there," a voice said from behind me. I turned to see Mr. Lunas standing there with a tiny sliver of a grin, his body not much bigger than a wisp of smoke.

"It would have been better if Ricky had built it. I don't even know if it will roll."

Mr. Lunas got down on his haunches and inspected my work. I swear I could hear his bones creak. "How are you going to steer it?"

I was so busy putting it together, I hadn't stopped to think of that. "I don't know."

He took off his hat and scratched his head. "I suspect if Ricky were making this, he'd loosen this front nail and steer this thing with his feet." He sat down on the back board and propped his feet up on each side of the front board. "See? You could push with your right foot to go left, and your left foot to go right."

It made sense to me. When he stood up, I grabbed the hammer and started jerking that nail out. Mr. Lunas cleared his throat, making a gruff, brittle sound. "Also," he went on, "since you already have a hole there from the nail, I bet you can put that large bolt in it and hold it on with that nut. But not too tight. It has to swivel, remember?"

Mr. Lunas was right. The bolt went in snug, but I worked the board back and forth, loosening it up enough to move with ease.

"And I think the same thing would go with those wheels too," he said. "Why not get those tight nails out of there and use those screws instead? You already have the holes to fit them."

Mr. Lunas guided me. I did all the work, and he did all the advising. He showed me what wrenches and screwdrivers to use. Another hour later, I sat down on the go-cart, imagining what it would be like to sail down the hill out front. I held my arms out to my sides as though I could feel the wind hitting my face.

"You're going to fall off if you ride like that," Mr. Lunas said, rubbing his chin.

He had a point. "What can I hold on to?"

He nodded toward some rope laying under the tree. "I think Ricky meant to use that. Tie each end on that front board, one on the left, one on the right. Tie it close to the main chassis. You can hold on to it like the reins on a horse."

I tied the rope tight, burning my hands with its coarse hairs. I tugged as hard as I could to make sure it didn't come loose. Then I sat on it again, feet up, reins in my hands. I swiveled the front board left and right to make sure it worked. It wasn't easy in the dirt, but on the open road, it would steer just fine. Hot dang, I'd built a go-cart!

I stood up and gave Mr. Lunas a proud smile. "Thank you. This'll work." And at the risk of crushing his feeble old bones, I gave him a super big, squeezy hug.

"Yep," he said, patting my back, then turning me loose. "That'll work just fine."

I let out a deep breath, feeling relieved and pleased with myself. "Hard part's over."

Mr. Lunas turned back toward the house. Without missing a step, he called over his shoulder, "Nope. Hard part is getting your brother outside to ride it."

Those words hit me like a baseball bat. My heart beat fast as I watched him hobble away, Buddy trotting right behind him. Mr. Lunas knew my secret! Now I just hoped and prayed he wouldn't tell a single soul.

Daddy cooked beans and corn bread for dinner that night. He heated up some tomato soup for Ricky. I watched him tiptoe to Ricky's bedroom door, set the bowl on the floor, then gently knock. He didn't bother hanging around to see if Mama would let him in.

I crumbled corn bread on my plate and covered it with a mountain of beans. Then I poured on extra bean juice. Daddy fixed his plate and sat down, and Mr. Lunas joined us, but he didn't eat.

"Mighty good beans," Daddy said to Mr. Lunas. "I'd hate for you to miss out." He shoveled some into his mouth, then swallowed it down with a big bite of corn bread.

Mr. Lunas shook his head. "Not hungry."

I couldn't bare to see him starve like this. "Maybe you should eat anyway. You can have some of mine."

His face brightened and his eyes twinkled like little stars. "Thank you, Janine, but I'll pass."

"Maybe dessert, then," I said, thinking how a big slice of pie would do him good.

He nodded. "Maybe."

Mr. Lunas tapped his bony fingers on the table while a stretch of quiet ran through the room. Then he spoke up again. "I'm leaving soon."

Daddy stopped chewing. So did I.

"Where are you going?" Daddy asked.

"Home."

Daddy laid down his fork with a loud chink. "Where's that?"

Mr. Lunas managed a crescent smile. "Up."

Daddy nodded. "Oh, Northerner. I didn't know that."

"I didn't either," I said. Mr. Lunas sure didn't talk like a Northerner. "Where up north—"

Mr. Lunas cut me off. "I'd sure like to say good-bye to Ricky before I go. I haven't seen him since he took ill."

Daddy let out one of those half-laughing, half-crying sounds I was getting used to.

"You can forget that. Adele's done barricaded the door. Ain't no one getting in there without a bulldozer."

"It doesn't seem healthy, does it?" Mr. Lunas said.

Daddy laid his head in his hand and rubbed his forehead. "What choice do I have? I can't offer a better solution."

I started thinking about my choices, too. Ricky has never been able to do what other kids do. No birthday parties or school field trips. And what good is someone's life if he can't do the *one* thing he really wants? *I have to find a way to break that barricade and give Ricky a ride on the go-cart. Somehow, some way. I just have to.*

☽

I spent most of the next morning making my plans and setting them into action. First I dragged the go-cart out front and hid it in the weeds by the side of the road. I needed it in place, in case I could manage to sneak Ricky out that night. I also hid some extra rope. Then I waited through the longest day of my life.

Mama stopped coming out of Ricky's bedroom,

even to use the bathroom. She just went in the same pot she had in there for him. Daddy set her iced tea and sandwiches by the door.

Around nightfall, I snuck out and peeked in Ricky's window. I could see with one eye through the slit in the curtains. He looked like a dried pepper, all withered up in the blanket. Mama sat with her Bible. Even though it was closed, she was hugging it close and mouthing words—Bible healing words, for sure. The door was blocked by a chest of drawers, and some dirty dishes sat on the floor by it. As I started to back away, something caught my eye—something I was sure Daddy didn't know about. The window was unlatched! I went around back and sat on the steps, watching Mr. Lunas hobble toward the cornfield with a handful of chicken eggs. More art supplies?

I sat for a long time in the darkness, wanting to plot my next move. But truthfully, I didn't have a clue what to do. Instead I imagined myself as a doctor, wearing a white coat with a silvery stethoscope around my neck. Nurses and orderlies move out of my way as I march down the sterile white halls of the hospital, on my way to an operating room where Ricky's waiting. I skillfully replace his gizzard, and then, after he's recovered, I hand him the key to his very own motor-powered go-cart. One that zooms like a jet. The entire hospital staff applauds.

I don't know how long I sat there in that dreamy fog, but I nearly jumped out of my skin when Mr. Lunas came up unnoticed and sat down next to me.

I wasn't sure if it was the darkness or his skin color that made him seem more like a shadow than a man. He looked like a stick with shoes on. And I just knew that if I accidentally touched him, he'd crumble into a little pile right there on the steps. No doubt about it, once I gave Ricky his go-cart ride, my new mission would be to get Mr. Lunas fattened up again.

He rubbed his face with his hands, saying, "I don't have much time."

I didn't know what he meant by that. Maybe

he was expected back home . . . wherever that was.

"Neither do I," I told him, wondering how many breaths Ricky had left. "Daddy says Ricky's going to die."

Mr. Lunas let out a sigh that was loud and wholehearted. "What can I tell you, Janine? People die. It's all a part of living."

"But he's too young! And he's never even had a chance at living." I was fighting tears and losing the battle. How could Mr. Lunas stay so calm?

"There's all kinds of living. Even a decade of being with people who love you, no matter where you go or what you do, can be all the living someone needs."

"Not Ricky," I argued. "He's going somewhere. And not just heaven."

He leaned toward me. "Are you going to do it tonight?"

I shook my head. "Mama's still awake. I don't think I can."

He reached over and patted my knee. "You'll think of something."

"I sure hope so."

He stood up to leave. "Yep. Hope is good."

☾

It rained the next morning. Not just a shower. Not even a thunderstorm. It was more like a cyclone. The house shook with the wildest gusts Texas could muster. Whirlwinds spun through the yard. Lightning streaked the quilted sky. And I hovered in my room, hoping the go-cart wasn't taking a beating. Mr. Lunas helped Daddy put the cows in the barn and cover the chicken coop with tarp. Buddy stayed put on the porch. Hailstones pounded the tin roof, and I imagined angry angels, frowning and throwing rocks at us. I wondered if this was the Bible plague Mama had seen in the tea leaves.

The storm knocked out all the electricity, so Daddy turned on a battery-powered radio to check the weather reports. "If you hear something that sounds like a train coming," he said, "jump in the bathtub and cover up with these blankets. You don't want to end up in Oz."

I didn't figure that was where I'd end up, and that had me worried. But I worried more about Ricky. What would Mama do if she heard a train coming?

I curled up in the cave and waited it out. It raged all day. At three o'clock, we still didn't have electricity, so I couldn't even pass the time watching afternoon cartoons. Late that night, the clouds shut off and drifted away, leaving twinkling stars above and gigantic puddles below. Like the lightning that had spiked around us all day, I felt charged up and ready for anything.

I waited until Daddy was snoring deep and loud before sneaking out. The grass was cold, wet and icky. I looked through the slit of the curtains into Ricky's room. He still laid there, the same as the night before. Mama laid next to him, sleeping, her mouth just slightly open.

I tried to open the window, but the heat and moisture had made the wood swell. The window was jammed. Buddy came around and jumped up on me with muddy paws. I was so aggravated that I pushed him down. "Buddy, if you're really smarter than people, then why don't you think of a way to get Ricky out?" He just tilted his head and stared.

I *had* to get that window open. I tugged again, and this time it slid up a bit. The opening was crooked, but I could slip my hands under it now. Taking my time, I inched it up little by little, one side, then the other. I didn't need to open it all the way, just enough so I could get in and out with Ricky. I pushed the curtains aside so I could have a better look around the room. All was quiet, hot, and sticky. I managed to slip the window up a little more, and Mama stirred. She rolled onto her side, facing the door. Just another inch, and I was in.

I tiptoed like a robber across the room. When I got to the bed, I moved Mama's Bible out of the way and gathered Ricky up in my arms. His eyes opened. I froze, afraid he'd say something and wake up Mama. But he smiled at me, then closed his eyes again. I tiptoed back to the window, holding Ricky like a tiny baby. He was as light as a kitten. Getting back out the window was the tricky part. But I did it without spilling my brother or myself on the ground. I took one look back inside. Mama hadn't moved a hair. I carefully took a few steps away, then ran toward the road, Buddy following.

Ricky bounced in my arms as I reached the weeds where I'd hidden the go-cart. I laid him down in the wet grass and dug the go-cart out. It had survived the storm, although it was plastered with damp weeds. I didn't care. It still rolled.

Buddy nudged at Ricky, wanting him to play. When Ricky didn't move, Buddy licked his hand.

I positioned the go-cart on the road at the top of the hill, then went back for Ricky. When I picked him up, he whispered, "Where are we?"

"Look," I said.

I tilted his head so that he could see the go-cart, and for a brief moment I saw his face light up. "I built it," he said, his words a real effort.

I set him down on the go-cart and placed the reins in his hands. "Try to hold on, okay?" I took the other piece of rope and tied it around his waist, then tied the ends to the go-cart. It held him up, even though he slumped forward.

"Are you ready?" I asked, wiping away a ribbon of blood that streamed from his nose.

He opened his eyes and looked out, down the hill toward the darkness.

I got behind him and whispered in his ear, "You're gonna race time, Ricky. You're gonna zoom. Ready . . . set . . ."

"Wait!"

I looked over to see Mr. Lunas limping toward us. Was he going to stop me or help me? I couldn't chance it.

"Go!" I gave the go-cart a hard shove and watched as it picked up speed, rolling down the steep road.

Ricky's head flew back as the go-cart whizzed on. It rushed straight down, and I imagined Ricky smiling all the way. But near the bottom, it veered to the left, running off the road through the gravel and slamming into a barbed-wire fence.

I suddenly felt as cold as the rain puddles. "Ricky!" I ran down the hill, racing toward him and the crashed go-cart. Fear tore at my heart. When I reached him, he was tangled in rope and fence. I picked a couple of barbs from his face and arms, untied him from the go-cart, and carried him to the road.

I sat down, hugging him, my tears spilling on his bloody face. His eyes opened for a moment, and he looked up at me. A small smile crossed his lips and he whispered, "Zoom." His eyes fluttered, rolled to white, and closed.

I hugged him tighter, rocking back and forth. He wasn't moving, not even a breath. Buddy whined. I cried. "Don't die, Ricky. Please . . . don't die."

Then two arms reached out to take him from me. Two thin, weak arms, not much bigger than Ricky's.

"No," I cried, squeezing Ricky tighter to my chest. "It's too late."

Mr. Lunas gazed at me, his eyes quivering. "Maybe not, but I need to hurry."

He reached again, and this time I handed my dead brother over to him. Mr. Lunas cradled Ricky, wiped some blood away, and whispered, "It's not your time to go." What I saw next made me wonder if I was awake or dreaming.

Mr. Lunas held his trembling hand just above Ricky's face. A small ball of light shone right out of his palm, faint at first, then glowing bright as a lantern. The light poured over Ricky like moonbeams over a field, brilliant and luminous. Buddy threw his head back and howled.

I looked close to see if Mr. Lunas was holding some kind of tiny flashlight, but beyond the blinding light, all I could see was his hand. A moment later, the light dimmed and went out.

Ricky rolled his head over and opened his eyes. He sat up, scratched his nose, looked around, and smiled.

I sat stiff and scared, trying like the dickens to believe what I'd just seen. When my mouth found the words, I finally asked, "Mr. Lunas? Uh—Uh— are you Jesus?"

He grinned, and in a strained voice he answered, "No, sweetheart, I'm not Jesus."

"Of course he's not Jesus," Ricky said, as perky as a pup. "His words aren't red!"

He and Mr. Lunas both chuckled at that, but I was still too stunned to move.

Ricky hopped up, adjusting his filthy pajamas. "Help me get my go-cart loose from the fence." He rushed over, tugging and pulling the stuck contraption. Buddy wagged his tail and barked as Ricky got the go-cart untangled. I didn't help. My mind was too full.

Mr. Lunas managed to stand up, but I imagined that any minute he might topple over like a row of dominoes. He was as weak as water. I wondered if he'd been this wilted to begin with, or if saving Ricky had zapped even more out of him.

Ricky tugged the go-cart behind him as he linked his arm through Mr. Lunas's to help him get up the hill. I found my feet and stood, then linked my arm on the other side, and together we managed to get Mr. Lunas back up to the house.

Ricky snuck back in the window. He promised to wait until I was safely inside to wake Mama up and show her his new strength. Still being Mr. Lunas's crutch, I helped him around to the porch.

"I'm not going in," he said as we got near the steps. "I've got to go."

His words swelled in my heart. "You can't go now! Not yet. I have a hundred million questions to ask you."

"I know you do, but it's impossible for me to stay any longer. I should've already been gone."

"But I don't understand," I said, rushing my words. "If you could use your hand like a magic wand, then why didn't you help Ricky before now? It sure would have saved us a lot of hoo-haw."

"Life is continually filled with hoo-haw," he said. "It's how we deal with it that defines who we are."

"But it don't make sense." *Would it ever?* "You could've shined that healing light on him the first night you came here. Why'd you put us through this?"

He rubbed his forehead, then faced me full-on. "It's hard to explain. Things come in cycles, like the seasons and the moon. I needed that cycle. Now my time is up."

He wobbled a little, and I clutched his arm tighter to hold him up.

"You're too sick to go anywhere," I said. "You just need to eat something. Let me go in and get you an apple."

He waved a hand to shush me. "An apple is not what I need."

"Then what *do* you need? I'll get it."

"I need to go home."

I didn't see how he'd get beyond the back-yard, much less somewhere up north. "You can go home tomorrow . . . after we celebrate Ricky not dying."

He shook his head. "I've done what I came to do, and I've plumb near overstayed."

What he came to do? To save Ricky? I leaned toward him and glared into his eyes. "Mr. Lunas . . . who *are* you?"

A grin replaced the grimace on his face. "I'm the soldier who saved your father in the war."

"And now you came to save my little brother."

His expression eased and he looked me in the eyes. "Who said it was your brother I came to save?"

I stared at his wilting gray face for a moment, trying to make sense of what he was saying. Then he looked beyond me toward the tall stalks of corn. "Tell your mama and daddy goodbye for me."

I nodded, still confused and trying to keep my tears at bay.

He tweaked my nose. "And tell Ricky I expect some great things from him."

"I'll tell him." I reached over and wrapped my arms around Mr. Lunas, giving him a hug so tight I might never let go. It was the biggest hug I'd ever given, and yet it didn't seem like enough. "Thank you. Thank you so much."

"No, thank *you*," he said, a slight twinkle making a glint in his eyes.

"For what? I didn't do anything."

"Oh yes, you did."

I must have looked as puzzled as I felt.

"Ricky was locked away, and getting past your

140

mother was going to take more strength than I had. You were my only hope. I may have saved Ricky's life, but you're the one who actually saved the day."

Although it was the dead of night, I must've been beaming brighter than the sun. I'd saved the day!

Mr. Lunas struggled with a few steps, then turned back one more time. "And by the way, I left you a little something."

"Really?" I said, truly beaming now. "What is it?"

"Something. Take good care of it."

"I will," I said, even though I hadn't a clue whether that was a promise I could keep.

"You know, Janine, I expect great things from you, too." He looked up at the sky, then back at me. "I'll be watching."

I couldn't help grinning inside and out. I just knew he was right. I would do great things too . . . one day.

Dark of the Moon

It'd been about a month since Ricky's recovery. Dr. Littlefield called it a miracle. Mama hugged her Bible and cried. Letting her believe her healing verses had cured Ricky seemed like the best thing to do. And besides, would she have believed me anyway?

Daddy parked right square in the middle of the drive-in movie lot, and Ricky and I stretched out on the hood of the car. With the sun sinking into pink ribbons behind the screen, it was just a matter of minutes before the movie started.

"Hey, knucklehead," I said, nudging Ricky and nearly making him spill his popcorn. "Don't you think it's weird?"

"What?" he answered, shaking the kernels off the side of the box.

"About Mr. Lunas. No one made the connection of him being there when Daddy got saved, and again when you were saved. You'd think they would have figured it out."

Ricky shrugged. "So?"

"You don't think Mr. Lunas had anything to do with you getting better?"

He shrugged again. "I don't know."

It struck me then that he *didn't* know. He didn't see what I saw, or know what I knew. It was going to be a secret I had to carry around all by myself.

Mama hopped up onto the car hood and bumped her hip against mine. "Scoot your butt over."

I let out a giggle while Ricky slapped his hand over his mouth. "Mmmmm . . . !" he snickered. "Mama said *butt*!"

I have to admit, it shocked me, too. This

from a woman who got mad if I said words like *golly* or *bullcorn*. *Butt* was downright unforgivable!

"Shush, Ricky," she said, grinning toward the screen. "I didn't give *you* permission to say it." She was grinning a lot more now.

"Why'd you come out here?" I asked Mama.

She squirmed a little closer. "It's too hot inside the car. And besides, that loose spring keeps poking my bu . . . behind."

There was a nice breeze sweeping the movie lot, and it cooled us down even though the hood was still warm from the drive over.

"Hey, Janine, catch!" Ricky tossed a piece of popcorn in the air and I caught it in my mouth. "My turn," he said, mouth wide.

I held one kernel between my fingers. He didn't see the others tucked into my palm.

"Hey!" he shouted when they all flew toward his face.

"Stop wasting that popcorn," Daddy called out. "Money don't grow on trees."

Nope, it didn't. It came from his new job at the warehouse.

About then, Daddy climbed out of the driver's-side door. "I can't see a thing. You're all blocking the windshield."

He scootched Ricky over, and we were jammed together like sardines.

"Ouch," Ricky whined. "You're crushing me." He crawled onto the car roof and laid down flat on his belly.

I stayed right where I was, in between Mama and Daddy. It felt nice. And we stayed that way all through the movie—from beginning to end.

☾

The nights became moonless and pitch dark again. I sat at my window, listening to the rustling in the cornfield. Was it the wind? Buddy sometimes went into the stalks for a while, but he always came out whining and sad. He'd lay in the dirt by my window and sulk. I'd seen some strange goings-on there this past month. Once I saw a

dust devil spiraling up, and for several nights t
lightning bugs swarmed with an endless, eei
glow. Tonight I could have sworn I heard the
cornfield calling my name. Somehow I wasn't
afraid. I grabbed a flashlight and headed out. I had
to see what was going on.

Buddy trailed behind me for a bit, then pushed
in front to lead the way. We squeezed between
stalks and leaves and yellow corn until we got to a
clearing—a perfect bald circle of dirt. I shined the
flashlight down for a better look. The circle was out-
lined with yellow pictures and stick figures that
looked like the Indian drawings found inside caves.
I studied them for a minute like a child looking at a
picture book. Some of them looked like the phases
of the moon. A moon that slowly turned into a
man, then circled back into the moon. Odd.

I also noticed a coffee can lying nearby, sur-
rounded by broken eggshells and some dried corn-
cobs. The person who drew this used egg yolks as
paint and the cobs as a brush. *Art supplies?*

I stepped into the middle of the circle and

closed my eyes, suddenly aware of the blood flowing through every vein in my body, from the large ones in my neck to the teeny ones in my toes. It rolled like a tide, rising and falling. Buddy curled up at my feet, and we stayed that way for a long time . . . until an owl called from a nearby tree, reminding me how late it was.

I passed Ricky's new and improved go-cart as I walked back to the house. He'd really worked hard, getting it fixed up. He finally admitted that I hadn't done such a bad job putting it together. I even took some turns riding it down the hill, cutting through the southern breeze. That go-cart really could zoom!

As I crawled into bed, I thought about Mr. Lunas and the cornfield, and my heart swelled a bit. I'd never see him again. Not the way he'd been this summer. Then I remembered a nursery rhyme that Mama used to recite to me when I was younger.

The man in the Moon looked out of the Moon,
Looked out of the Moon and said,

> " 'Tis time for all children on the earth
> To think about getting to bed."

The August heat was too much, so I drew just a thin sheet up over me for covers. I closed my eyes and steadied my breathing. Being so tired, I figured sleep would come right away, but my mind kept going back to that cornfield. I tossed and turned, a small light aggravating my eyes. I reached over to switch off the lamp, but it was already out.

I shot up quickly, looking around. Where was that dang light coming from? Then I found it . . . up under the sheet! It was just a small glow, about the size of a walnut, shining from the palm of my hand. I gasped and flinched, one heartbeat away from fear. Then I squeezed it a few times, watching the beams seep through my fingers. It didn't hurt a bit. Actually, it felt pretty natural. The biggest smile ever busted out across my face.

I scrunched back down onto my pillow, hugging my hand close to my heart. Mr. Lunas had said he'd left me something. He had. He had indeed.

Moon Facts

☾ The moon is about 225,745 miles from Earth.

☾ It takes the moon twenty-nine and a half days to orbit Earth.

☾ The new moon always rises at sunrise, the first quarter moon at noon. The full moon rises at sunset, the last quarter moon at midnight.

☾ "Blood around the moon" is an atmospheric condition produced by high, thin clouds.

☾ The moon affects the ocean tides (because of its magnetic pull) and the hunting habits of nocturnal animals.

☾ *Luna* is the Latin word for *moon*.

☾ The August moon is called the full corn moon.

☾ A blue moon is a second full moon in a calendar month.

☾ During an address to Congress on May 25, 1961, President John F. Kennedy stated: "First, I believe that this nation should commit itself to achieving the goal, before this decade is out, of landing a man on the moon and returning him safely to the earth." On July 20, 1969, *Apollo 11*, with astronauts Michael Collins, Neil Armstrong, and Buzz Aldrin, successfully landed on the moon.

☾ The Man in the Moon does exist. Look up on a moonlit night and make a wish.

About the Author

Dotti Enderle is the author of numerous books for children and educators, including the Fortune Tellers Club series, *Grandpa for Sale* (cowritten with Vicki Sansum), and *The Cotton Candy Catastrophe at the Texas State Fair*. As a professional storyteller, she has entertained at numerous schools, libraries, museums, and festivals since 1993. A native Texan, she lives with her family in Houston. Visit her at www.dottienderle.com.